IMP AND THE DARKSERPENT

DONNIE BARTON

Enjoy the adventure,

Donnie B.

IMP AND THE DARKSERPENT

Donnie Barton

Published 2018 by Donnie Barton

Copyright 2018 by Donnie Barton

Printed in the United States of America

"Uso nepherell," yelled Lira, as her tiny trembling fingers sketched the last of the magical runes into the air. The small Hauflin sorceress stood as threads of magic coalesced into a swirling portal of arcane power. Holding her swollen stomach, she stepped into the portal as the maelstrom of arcane energy passed over the Tower of Kalos. Her body stung as arcane energies of the storm scalded her tiny body. Falling, falling through the eternity of a heartbeat, Lira fell towards a shimmering light, then darkness.

Neelia stood lost in silent contemplation as she slowly crushed the crimson blossoms of the witch's heartblood vine in her mortar. Through the years, she had meticulously grown accustomed to using the old marbled pestle, now stained by the numerous herbs ground over time. Pale rays of moonlight fought through the clouds as the storm settled past the city. Sheets of lightning lit the distant skyline, leaving only the faintest sign of static in the air. The flowers in the garden danced with the shadows, as the drops of rain water sparkled in the soft moonlight.

Neelia's son Edwyn played near the small hearth, which Neelia used occasionally to dry her newly grown herbs. Dark curly hair and even darker eyes, Edwyn had barely seen his third year before they had left her childhood home in the Green Forest, where she and her lost love had embraced the natural wonders of the world. Now five years of age, he was the only treasure to remind her of her past life, a young mirror image of her husband, Jerrod.

From outside on the balcony, small orbs of light seemed to flash into and out of existence. Looking out of the window into the darkness Neelia watched these small apparitions come and go as fireflies in the night. She sat down her pestle and slowly made her way to the balcony door. Cautiously she opened the wooden door and peeked quietly out upon the balcony. Not a light of any kind could be seen flying through the moonlit sky. Bolstering her courage, Neelia stepped out amongst her flowers and herbs. The garden seemed eerily quiet as she stood looking from side to side, and then scanning the alley below. Deciding she had only imagined the occurrence, Neelia began to pass back through the doorway as the leaves of the Shadowtop next to her shop began to rustle. The ghostly orbs seemed to appear from nothingness and flew around her like tiny hummingbirds looking for nectar. As she marveled at the small wisps surrounding the balcony, she was alerted by the breaking of her small ceramic pots as they shattered on the boards. Then suddenly, with a flash of intense blue light and the low grumble of thunder, Neelia, found herself knocked to the balcony floor. Rising to a sitting position, she slowly rubbed the blurriness from her eyes. The only orbs left she now saw danced on the edge of her vision. As Neelia, somewhat shaken, began to rise to her feet something caught her eye.

From under a pile of broken pots and withered creeper vines, she saw a tiny hand that seemed to be curled in agony. With the handle of the old straw broom that lay dormant on the tattered boards of the balcony, she slowly pushed the broken pottery and withered greenery out of the way to gain a better view of what seemed to laying beneath the rubble. Astonished, as well as amazed, the apothecary discovered the form of a small woman. With trembling hands, the aging widow reached out and touched her tiny visitor. The Hauflin's skin seemed to smolder as if the tiny creature was on fire. Breathing slowly, the apothecary tried to control her own trembling hands as she scooped up the tiny being. As Neelia started to rise anxiously to her feet, the tiny woman opened her sea blue eyes. And with a sigh they closed again.

Lira opened her eyes to the sound of humming and a cool dampness on her forehead. Her skin felt as if she had stayed out in the desert sun far too long. The room was sparsely lit by only a few candles, but it was much larger than her old house back in the Burrows. A Bigg, stood over a basin of water ringing out numerous strips of tattered cloth. Then the pain hit again. Lira clutched her small stomach, and gasped as her muscles seemed to contract. Lira breathed heavily as the contractions became more pronounced. "My baby, comes," was all Lira could exasperate fearfully as her eyes began to glow with a ghostly blue light. Small wisps of magical light appeared, moving to and fro around the room.

The Bigg turned to reveal the visage of an older human female with a kind face and gentle eyes. "Calm your heart, tiny one," the human said while placing a gentle hand upon Lira's trembling stomach, "save your strength for you will need it."

Lira could feel a calmness touch her mind as the woman began to hum. With every contraction, tiny blue runes appeared on her belly illuminating the contracting muscles. Her blood burned with the old world's arcane energy causing her skin to smolder again drying the dampness from the soaked rags. Breathing hard and pushing harder, Lira tried to concentrate on the beating of her own tiny heart and the rhythm of the woman's humming. But she soon grew tired, managing one final strong push. And then she finally heard the small cry of her child. Turning with the infant in hand, Neelia, cradled the newborn carefully presenting it to its exhausted mother. Lira, exhausted and worn, looked upon her son, wrapped in old rags, and stretched her shivering hand out to hold his. A tiny perfect hand. Then as if on cue, with a sigh and a glowing tear Lira closed her eyes.

"Rest now my darling," the woman said as the lights swirled into memory, dimming as the mother passed from this world to the next.

CHAPTER ONE

*P*ulling his small ash colored cloak tighter, Keebo sat on the crumbling stone ledge facing the tavern, The Smitten Siren. He had waited patiently over the last few nights for the moment when he would be able to teach the young lord a final lesson on the mistreatment of the small folk. But tonight, as drops of a cool summer rain gently fell, he watched for the young Lord Tunstall to depart from his nightly debauchery. The young lad's attitude when dealing with the small folk had turned into blatant bullying of his aging father's loyal customers.

Finally as the clock tower tolled two bells, the door of the tavern flew open as the Lord Tunstall stumbled out, cursing the watered down ale and making a mockery of the serving wenches and himself. Constantly looking toward the sky, the young lord stumbled to his horse, pulling his cloak tightly to protect against the dampness.

"Disgusting," Keebo silently whispered to himself as the lord missed the stirrup when trying to mount his horse, "such a noble display of a noble upbringing." Keebo turned his head and spat to the cobblestone streets below, which had started to become overrun by the fog that had crept in from the surrounding docks. Watching the noble, who had finally balanced himself in his handsomely adorned saddle, Keebo climbed to his feet. It felt good to be off of the damp ledge as he stretched his small bat-like wings to the sky. The tiny veins seemed to glow with iridescent blue in anticipation, as the adrenaline started to pump from his pint-sized Hauflin heart. Pulling his leather mask down, he assumed the visage of an infernal creature stalking his prey. And with a flap of his wings, the young vigilante took to the air after the young nobleman.

Gliding from roof top to roof top, Keebo watched as the young lord's horse swayed in the ghost-like fog. The lord had definitely filled his gullet to the point that his coordination had diminished to mere nothingness. He had decided to put his plan into action. Jumping from the roof top he had recently landed upon, he soared high above the two story stone buildings as the lord made his way up Downwater Street. And then, as Keebo attained the apex, he twisted and dived toward the unsuspecting rider. Screeching as he plummeted toward his prey, he could almost see the hairs on Tunstall's neck rise. Hands shaking, he shuddered as it took all his concentration not to lose his grasp on his steed. Tunstall scanned the sky, looking for the shadowy creature that had the audacity to harass one of noble blood, or as noble as one of the up and coming merchant houses could be. And then again, the shadow soared passed the lord, shrieking as it passed.

"Come out, damn you," The Lordling exclaimed, his hands visibly trembling, one hand on the reins, one on his pommel, "Face me, Coward!" But way down deep in the young lord's soul, he prayed that whatever it was would just leave him be.

Finally nearing the end of the fog-laden cobblestone street, Keebo made his final pass, but this time his target was not the shivering lord, but his nervous steed. Soaring low, Keebo flew past the horse level with it flanks, and with a mighty screech panicked the creature into throwing his master. With a loud thump, the lordling landed on the damp cobblestone street, bouncing to a sudden stop. Keebo observed him from the iron lamppost he had come to land on. He had curled his tail around the post to keep himself from losing his footing as he perched on the rain-soaked metal. The flickering of the lamp's green flame caused shadows to eerily distort Keebo's features, adding to his infernal illusion.

The young lord sat dazed as he grasped his ribs that had been cracked in the fall. As the stars cleared from the edge of his vision, he began to focus on the creature staring down at him from the lamppost.

"You have angered the gods, whelp, and I have been sent to claim your soul. You have shown no respect to those of the Burrows, of whom you have greedily taken hard earned coin and treat so terribly. Have you learned not a single lesson from your fair and noble father?" Keebo said with a fearsome sneer.

As with most nobles, this one thought he was above the laws of common courtesy that most commoners were born with. Trying to prove his bravado, he tried to rise to his feet, already feeling for the pommel of his rapier. Keebo lunged from the lamppost, adding his position and the height to his momentum as he plowed head first into the drunk excuse of a lord, driving him back to the ground. Burying the heel of his worn leather boot into the cracked ribs of the drunken youngling,

Keebo planted his other in the soft underside of the drunkard's chin. He could smell the stale ale on the lord's breath and the possible stench of urine. How the mighty have fallen, thought Keebo, as he grabbed his prey's worn silk collar. Sounds of heavy boots coming down the cobblestone street caused the small assailant to look over his shoulder. He could make out the faint green light of the city watch's lanterns. He would have to shorten this purposed intervention but maybe it had been enough. Piercing silvery blue eyes illuminated the leather mask, as he peered into the lord's eyes.

"You are cursed Lord Tunstall, respect the small folk, or your soul is forfeit. The gods are watching!" Keebo stated with a dire conviction. And with a quick kick to the jaw, he spread his leathery wings and ascended into the darkness.

Green light flooded the area, as the watch encountered the scene. Walking to the young man, the graying captain cautiously scanned the street. All he discovered was the seemingly drunken man sitting in the street, who looked as if he had been on the losing end of a good scrap. With the strong smell of ale, the lordling sat trembling on the wet cobbles, clutching his aching side mumbling incoherently the words "cursed and demon". The captain, recognizing the youth's family crest, had two of his watchman escort the bruised and battered young noble back home to the safety of his manor's walls. The watch didn't need any more problems around the docks than what was already there, especially noble problems.

Flying over the wall that separated the docks and the rest of Stormhaven, Keebo made his way to the rear of a small two story rough cut stone building, with terracotta shingles. Planters filled with numerous herbs and flowers portrayed a well-kept garden situated on the small balcony covering the rear entrance. Alighting on the tiny ledge just below the roof, Keebo drearily scanned the alley before he slowly pushed open the small circular stained glass window. The warm air, scented by drying lavender, felt welcomed compared to the cool rain drizzling outside. Keebo quietly climbed through the window, which opened into a small lofty room, furnished as any child's bedchamber would be. Dropping his leather jerkin to the floor and placing his fiendish mask into the small alcove behind his dresser, he climbed into his warm and inviting bed. With thoughts of fleeting retribution, he fell into a well-earned sleep.

KEEPING TO THE SHADOWS, Tinker slowly

made his way down the stone alley way connecting Toad 'n' hole to Sparkling Rocks, a street so named for the sand quartz that sparkled when light hit it. The alleyway, like most of the streets in the Burrows, was nearly five feet high and seven feet at its widest. Beyond the streets, houses and shops made the walls that held these vast tunnels upright. His well-oiled leather boots muffled most of the sound as he tried to keep up with the two hairy Gnomes. He had followed them ever since he had spotted the unusual pair exiting the Deep Burrow entrance that led to the lowest and oldest levels of the Burrows. They carried something, something that caused them to stay in the shadows themselves. Making his way quietly to the corner, he carefully peeked around, spying the two eyeing the street. Straining his tiny ears he could hear them talking.

"Where we take him?" asked the shorter of the two, readjusting the weight of the bundle in his arms. "He's get'en heavy!"

"Shut up, Tunks!" snarled the taller scraggly Gnome. "Boss said put'em back where we got him. So shut up, the Watch is coming. Put him down and hide us why don't you!"

Lowering the bundle to the ground, Tunks slowly crossed his gnarled fingers and moved them haphazardly above him as if drawing some form of crude symbol in the air. As the Watch grew closer the air in front of the two Gnomes seem to ripple the tiniest amount. The faint glow of the Watch's lantern, carried by a dwarf and Hauflin garbed in scarlet red tabards, bathed the walls of Sparkling Rocks in green light causing them to twinkle. Passing the entrance to the alley, the red haired dwarf turned and surveyed the darkened alley. Tinker finally realized that the watchman couldn't see the two Gnomes, who were now standing motionless at the end of the alley, for he looked past them into the darkness. Scratching his bearded chin and taking a second glance, the Dwarven watchman turned forward again and with his companion resumed their patrol.

Chancing a glance around the stone laden corner, Tinker watched as the two Gnomes slipped out of the alley and down the slightly sloping street. Moving as quickly and as quietly as possible, he crept to the opening of the alley. Hugging the wall, he peeked around the corner and down the street trying to spot his mysterious friends. The street was on average five to six feet tall and ten feet at its widest. Numerous stairs leading up and down led to other levels as streets and alleys intersected. Magical fire danced in the orbs lighting the street. Few small folk roamed the streets at night and the Watch made their rounds on schedule. Moving quickly, the young Hauflin moved down the street, checking stairs and alcoves, until he happened upon Hobbler's Junction, an intersection where numerous traders and businesses were located. The junction seemed deserted, except for a few traders unloading their crates from a small two wheeled cart. They noticed Tinker, but didn't show much concern for the youth.

Spotting the two Gnomes across the junction, Tinker increased his speed, drawing power from his unusual gift that affected his metabolism. What were they up to he wondered, his curiosity getting the better of caution. Through an ornate stone archway, that helped support the upper levels, Tinker made his way after them. Rounding a corner, he stumbled, barely catching himself. Crouching down, he focused on the taller of the two Gnomes kneeling down, who started to untie the bundle. Inside, swaddled in the burlap cocoon, was an aging Hauflin man. After removing the cloth, the Gnome pulled the Hauflin up next to the door of a small but quaint little bakery. Tinker thought to himself how odd this all seemed. This man was an ordinary baker, although his goods were some of the best in the Burrows. The Hauflin was still just a baker.

Lost in his thoughts, Tinker finally realized that

the Gnome was looking in his direction. Not only in his direction, but his beady little eyes were trained directly on him. Then it donned on him, the other Gnome. Adrenaline rushed through every tiny artery as he realized his folly. A shiver ran over him as the stale breath of the other Gnome warmed his neck. Reaching into his leather jerkin, the young Hauflin reached for his trusty dagger. Taking a deep calming breath, Tinker spun around on his heels only to meet the brutal end of a sap. The Gnome's iron filled leather sap, hit with a force making a wet bludgeoning sound as it connected with the Hauflin's head. Feeling the warm blood start to ooze from his head, stars started to develop in the youth's blurry vision. He tried to gain his bearing. But then the floor of the street rushed up to meet boy, as his wobbly legs gave way and darkness consumed him. Moments, maybe hours passed as Tinker found himself being wrapped in the same burlap cocoon. Mind still going in and out of consciousness, as the world faded in and out from view, pictures raced like broken dreams. Eyes fluttering, opening momentarily to catch one last sight, the toothy smile of a scraggly Gnome pulling the burlap cloth over his face.

BLURRED SHADOWS DANCED on the edge of Tinker's sight as he slowly regained his consciousness. Two figures stood before a stone alter, one cloaked, one scraggly, talking in muffled voices as the cloaked figure reached for a wicked athame. Dragging the curved blade through the flesh of his viciously clawed hand, the cloaked figure in silence, clenched his fist allowing his blood to trickle from the cut into a cracked flask. The young Hauflin's head ached, and he knew he didn't want to be on the business end of that dagger. Tinker tried to move, but his wrists and ankles were held tightly behind the chair that he sat in. That was when the chair slightly made a shuffling sound on the stone floor. Thinking to himself "the Hells," Tinker tried to play possum.

Dipping the dagger's blade in the blood, the cloaked man dribbled a few drops of the dark red gore into the concoction that sat bubbling over the small open flame.

"AHHHH, I see our young friend is awake," stated the cloaked figure as his back straightened. Then he turned revealing eyes that seemed to shine like rubies in the candle light. "No need for the illusion, your breathing betrays you, young one."

Tinker raised his head and coldly stared at the

two men. The scraggly haired Gnome moved toward Tinker, standing directly behind him. His clothes were torn and in desperate need of repair. The stench of fresh dung stung Tinker's nose and lungs. Tinker fought the bile rising in his throat, fighting the feeling to wretch.

"Want me kill, boss?" said the scraggly Gnome, as he ran his grimy hand through Tinker's hair, intertwining his gnarled fingers around a tuft of long hair. Then suddenly the Gnome yanked Tinker's head back.

"Tsk ,tsk. Now Nip, is that any way to treat such a ... a special boy, a kindred spirit? Won't you be a good boy and tell me why you were following O'l Nip there?" stated the cloaked figure. "Maybe we'll let you go then, maybe."

"Good sir, you must be mistaken, I don't know nothing. I have never seen this man before," stated Tinker as he gave the cloaked man an innocent smile that was short lived. For all of the sudden, Tinker's head was wrenched back again, making way for a scraggly fist to be planted along the young Hauflin's jaw line. A trickle of blood ran down his chin as he spit toward the cloaked figure. "To the Hells with you and your dog, you bastard!" spat Tinker as another strike landed on his jaw.

Throwing his hood back, the figure turned revealing not the visage of a Hauflin, but a rat-like creature. Blood red eyes shined in the candlelight as his whiskers moved ever so dauntingly. In his hand a huge ladle, that had been filled from the bubbling concoction that sat on the table. Inching ever closer the cloaked figure moved toward the bound youngling as Tinker tried to break his bonds, straining every aching muscle. Grabbing the young Hauflin's throat, the cloaked figure's clawed hand slowly moved to Tinker's swollen jaw. Squeezing his mouth open, the cloaked figure forced the ladle between Tinker's clutched teeth allowing for the congealing liquid to ooze down into his gullet. Tinker started to gag as the thickening liquid slowly seeped into his stomach, the cloaked figure held the young bound Hauflin's nose and mouth to make sure that he kept it down. Gurgling noises erupted from deep within the captive's stomach. Flushed skin followed by an agonizing look as pain wracked the Hauflin's small body.

"WH-what have you dun to me?" Tinker slurred as stars began to twinkle on the edge of his vision. Trying to shake off the mind-numbing effects, he could feel his body floating, floating ever higher. Head lulling to one side again he slurred "WH-wh-wha you to me." Eyelids slowly lowering as his mind drifted further and further, the young

Hauflin finally succumbed to the welcoming darkness.

LIGHT FOOTSTEPS COULD BE HEARD COMING and going down the hall, as Thucious studied the broadsheets lying on his desk. Line after line, sheet after sheet, he ran his six fingered hand across them looking for any interesting story that might contain even the tiniest drop of truth. Thucious was in the information business, and had been for a long time. Stormhaven had become his mistress, and in his eyes, information, scandalous or otherwise, had become her life's blood. It had taken many years to develop his network of knowledge seekers, especially after magic had become so untrustworthy as of late. He often sat at his desk, reminiscing about the days before the threads of magic had been unraveled, the days that even his own god walked the world. But now he had to stay more vigilant as Stormhaven had evolved and grew to a woman, not the young girl he once fell in love with.

A knock on the old wooden door frame brought Thucious out of his perpetual daydream. His senses returning, he looked back to the broadsheets as Filpin entered the office struggling to carry a stack of ledgers and scrolls.

"Morning boss, I have the rosters and schedules for you," stated Filpin hesitantly as he came into the office. Filpin was a lanky human youth, with small wire rimmed spectacles, who had a particular comprehension for numbers. He had barely seen his tenth season when he had been discovered wandering the streets by Thucious. Now at the age of sixteen years, he helped to manage the courier business that had given Thucious his first foothold in Stormhaven.

Filpin pushed the ledgers on the desk as sweat beaded along his brow. "No broadsheet from the docks this morning?" asked Thucious as he started to go over the daily log of deliveries.

"Beg your pardon, sir! The sheet arrived a little later than normal, Tinker didn't show up this morning for breakfast or work, so I had to send one of the younger runners for it today, and they had a hard time finding the crier."

Odd Thucious thought, as Hauflins go, Tinker was always quite punctual and rarely missed a meal. The lanky boy stood patiently by as Thucious scoured the rosters and ledgers, examining his young assistant's handy work. Filpin was meticulous in every detail, yet he lacked the confidence that would only come with age.

Flipping sporadically through the ledgers, Thucious made a point to verbally emphasize some detail with a slight "Mhmm or a yes indeed," before he closed them and passed them back to his young upstart with a nod. And with a "well done," Thucious picked up the newest broadsheet, and began to skim the headlines.

"**BEWARE OF IMPS**," seemed to scream to the reader in great bold letters. Definitely meant to capture the reader's eye and hold on to their full attention, Thucious read on.

BEWARE OF IMPS!

A brave lord was attacked by numerous demonic imps last eve along the docks. The lord had been discovered by the Watch after the desperate lad had battled numerous infernal creatures in an attempt to steal his soul. Surrounded by numerous dead creatures of the Nine Hells, near death and wounded severely, the Watch escorted the noble lord, back to his estate. The Lord stated that after handling such a barrage of fiends, he would heal in the comfort of his own manor instead of the nearest temple. So as a warning to all, beware ye all weary travelers.

Although magic in the past sometimes

wavered, the alarms put in place around the docks seemed to not be faltering. Of course they had been cast many years before the great wars of magic and held the same degree of arcane potency as when set into place. Thucious would have known if one of the infernal creatures were running around that part of the city. He would have to take a stroll later and reexamine the glyphs.

THE SMELLS of fried pork and biscuits wafted up through the old stone chimney, to the nose of the unsuspecting creature curled up under the old rabbit fur blanket and a tattered patchwork quilt. A rumbling growl escaped from beneath the mismatched rabbit fur. First a shudder, and then a shake as tiny hands reached out and grasped the edge of the blanket. Then slowly a head emerged from its hidden burrow. With a great yawn, Keebo opened his cerulean eyes. It had been a rough night and the morning had arrived too early as the clock tower tolled seventh hour. But breakfast was too important to be missed, especially at the thought that dinner was so far away. Dangling his legs over the side of the bed, he sat up stretching, first his tiny arms and then his regal wings.

Slowly, with half-lidded eyes, Keebo barely made it to the floor from his bed. Stepping off the small step ladder, he cautiously placed one foot after the other on the cold wooden boards of the floor. With a shiver, Keebo slowly made his way to the wash basin setting on a salvaged crate near the door. "Yeow," he exclaimed as he splashed his face with the cold water from the pitcher. Reaching into the dresser, he fished out a pair of breeches and an old shirt belonging to his brother. Luckily for him, his big brother Edwyn, was a Bigg. So any hand me down shirts would help hide his wings, or any attributes that most folks would consider out of the ordinary. Pulling the small leather strap through the silver buckle, he fastened his wings tightly against his back using the special harness his brother had devised. Then he donned Edwyn's shirt, which looked only the slightest disproportion. Tightening his belt and pulling on his worn leather boots, he opened the door to the smell of breakfast and business.

Mother had seen to it that all of the doors had a smaller door built into them. Heading down the hallway and past Edwyn's room, he could hear his older brother talking to the patrons that had come to do business at the Green Forest. Mother had owned the apothecary shop, until her recent passing, in which the business was left in the caring hands of Edwyn. Her wares were sought out from every corner of the city, and although she had made only enough gold to support her and her children, her true wealth came from the knowledge that she passed on to everyone who met her.

Walking down the curved staircase, Keebo paused momentarily, watching the patrons roam around the bundles of dry herbs and shelves of ointments shoved together on tightly packed shelves. A young noble stared at the floor, unable to make eye contact, as Edwyn held a small clay jar of ointment and explained how to apply it. Edwyn glanced up at his little brother giving him a sly wink as he returned his attention to the worried lad who kept shifting his weight from one foot to the other.

A growl rose from Keebo's stomach, reminding him of the first task of the day, finding the remainder of the biscuits and fried pork. Following the stairs, he made his way into the drying room that contained the hearth that would serve also as a kitchen. Placed on the table sat a plate with two biscuits and fresh fried pork that his brother had cooked early that morning. The plate set next to a stack of orders that his brother had started acquiring the ingredients to create. The room was filled with numerous bundles of herbs and roots hanging from the ceiling to dry. Fancy glass bottles were crowded together, with numerous odd shaped clay jars containing various liquids and specialty ingredients.

Tearing a biscuit in two halves, the fragrant smell of the fresh honey that his brother mixed in the dough filled his tiny nostrils. Breathing deeply, a smile settled over his lips as he then grabbed a piece of pork, placing it between the two halves. It tasted so good, the sweetness of the biscuit and the crunch of the pork, every bite left his mouth watering, craving more. This was definitely worth waking up for this morning.

Almost to paradise, Keebo crept closer with every heavenly bite and then, he could hear his brother yelling for him from the next room.

"Keebs," yelled his brother as he tossed the last scrumptious morsel into his mouth. Retrieving his apron from the hook on the wall, he looped it over his head and tied it around his back as he exited the back room into the store. Edwyn smiled as he nodded in the direction of some small folk who looked a little exasperated while examining numerous jars of ingredients. Keebo walked from around the counter, which had a portion made especially for their customers of the small folk persuasion, and waded himself through the aisles.

"Good morrow, sir," Keebo said as he eyed gray haired Hauflin whose eyes seemed full of worry,

"Welcome to the Green Forest, home of the finest apothecary in the city, perhaps all the world. How can we be of service to you this fine day?"

"I am Timbles, Timbles Tallbreeches and I come here beseeching a cure. My beloved is not well, she seems to burn with the fever and hasn't been her happy self in many a day. I fear she is getting worse!" The older Hauflin said as his eyes seem to fill with water. Keebo had seen sad Hauflins before, but usually they were never so melancholy. They must have been together a long time he quietly thought.

Keebo placed his hand on the old man's shoulder as he led him to the counter where a tiny stool stood. Taking out a piece of parchment, he started to note in detail each ailment that seemed to be besetting his lady. He took care to have the old man elaborate as much as possible any characteristics that would help identify her affliction. After finishing taking notes, Keebo turned and knelt down as he retrieved a small leather bound journal with numerous markers jutting out of the pages. He turned page after page trying to identify certain ingredients that would cure the ailments suffered by his wife. He would make notations of the ingredients he would mix together. Blue Barrow root for the headache, ash of Briarwood for the cough, and oil of the Cephran flower to regain strength, but he couldn't identify any information covering darkening skin. Reaching up and tugging at the hem of Edwyn's apron, he held the list of maladies for his brother to identify. Examining the list, Edwyn knelt down to meet the old man's eyes.

"I am sorry your lady has been ill of late, but it seems that we can remedy all but one of her maladies," Edwyn stated with a sincere look in his eyes. "When did her skin start to look different?"

The tiny old man placed a weathered hand to his chin and thought. "It started about a half a tenday ago, slowly at first but more hurriedly as her fever progressed. We have tried everything. Our tailoring business had been slow for a while and we couldn't afford magical healing. The healers at the temple haven't been able to cure her ailments nor have our own apothecaries, so we have sought a cure among the Biggs."

Edwyn scribbled his notes, taking time to ponder each ingredient. Then he turned and passed through the heavy, green curtain embroidered with a golden tree that separated the back room and the front of the store. Setting his notes on the table, he started to gather the ingredients from around the room. He selected a young piece of Blue Barrow root that would help ease the blood flow to the mind reducing her headache. From a shelf, he picked out a small red clay jar of Briarwood ash to stifle her coughing fits. And then he walked over to a vine covered ornate cabinet that contained numerous glass vials. Gently opening the small glass doors, Edwyn carefully reached in and picked up the translucent lavender oil of the Cephran flower. This one oil made most of the others in the cabinet pale in comparison. The tiniest drop of the flower's nectar brought on the effects of renewed vitality. It was quite costly and had been secreted away from the jungles of Jesec by an overly ambitious adventurer.

He started to meticulously slice the barrow root into pieces before he placed them in the mortar. Adding two heaping spoonfuls of the briarwood ash, Edwyn slowly pressed down on the pestle and coaxed the juices from the roots out to mingle with the ash forming a pasty concoction. Then ever so gently he added a single drop from the vial into the mortar. The smell of the oil itself wafted up into his nostrils, silently whispering of its vitality. From there, the mixture would be mixed with spring water and boiled down into a thick elixir that could be swallowed easily. Removing the bubbling remedy from the flame, Edwyn slowly poured it through a cheese cloth, allowing only the liquid to fill the tiny bottle. Tightly stoppering the bottle, he made his way back to the counter and the eagerly waiting old man.

"Take this and give it to her three times a day," stated Edwyn as he wrapped the small bottle in a stout cloth. "It should help with most of the maladies, but what affects her skin I would need to research."

Timbles nodded as he tried to commit the directions to memory, then he pulled out a small cloth pouch from under his vest. Shaking it gently, he could hear what few coins he had jingle as they bounced off each other. Placing the money bag on the counter, he weighed the contents against the elixir in the small bottle. Sighing Timbles muttered that no amount was too great. Edwyn looked at the old man, then at his little brother, placing his hand on the little bag of coins. Looking at his brother, Edwyn pushed it back toward the aging Hauflin.

"This will not do, this elixir contains a costly oil and is very expensive to procure," stated Edwyn at the now exasperated old man, "That amount of coin will not come close to the amount we are in need of."

"That is all I can afford" Timbles said in a trembling voice, "I can try to find more but I barely can feed my family now." It was true that a Hauflin's family could be rather large at times. Timbles started to tuck the small bag back into his belt as Edwyn placed a gentle hand on his patron's small shoulder.

"I think on this occasion," as he pressed the small package into the Hauflin's hand, "a better deal could be made. My brother could really use a new pair of breeches or maybe a shirt. How about a trade?"

The Hauflin carefully eyed the human with a puzzled look. He sat there thinking of what trick the Bigg was trying to pull when Keebo spoke up.

"That sounds like a great idea, brother. I could really use some breeches or perhaps a new cloak, mine is quite worn. I could also check on your lady and see if her condition has worsened," stated Keebo as if examining the torn breeches he now wore.

Timbles stuck his tiny hand out and clasped Edwyn and Keebo's hands. Then he grabbed the small bottle and headed to the door. Turning and waving, he disappeared out into the street. The two brothers looked at each other with big smiles as they prepared for any new patrons to visit the Green Forest. Mother had always taught them to help those in need, regardless of bags of gold or chests of treasures. And they did.

The day went on and as the afternoon lingered, the stack of orders diminished into deliveries to be made. Keebo loved the afternoons when Edwyn would send him near and far to deliver their concoctions to patrons all around the city. Hanging his apron back on the hook in the back room, he would then don his brother's old haversack. It was a little bulky and smelled of worn leather, but it allowed for him to slightly loosen the leather strap holding his wings tightly against his back. Packing the bundles in the numerous pockets contained within the haversack, Keebo was soon on his way.

A cool breeze blew off of the waves that swayed in and out of the harbor. The sun hung brightly in the western sky just four bells past the noon day sun as Keebo made his way amongst the noble manors. He enjoyed the walk, although he preferred to be soaring past the nobles' manors with their great twisting spires. He was free then, spiraling through the sky, not a care in the world. Down the cobblestone street he traveled, the warm heat still coming off of the stones as he dodged the noble lords and ladies, who paid no attention to those on foot, and especially none as small as himself. But when he was noticed by the Biggs, he grinned wholeheartedly as they always patted themselves down for any missing items. He was a well-know and accomplished apothecary, or at least his brother was, with a legitimate trade. How typical of the Biggs he thought, as he arrived at his destination.

Shielding his eyes with a tiny hand, he looked up at the colorful metal sign hanging over the entrance to the shop; Keebo breathed his own little sigh of relief. The sign's enchantment made the **Glimmering Adornments** seem to sparkle even as the rays of the setting sun no longer graced its presence. This shop catered to the tall and mighty, as one would assume, due to no small folk door. He stretched his Hauflin arm as far as he could while standing on his tippy toes. Barely touching the latch of the painted wooden door, he gave it a good tug, causing the chimes to announce his entrance into the store. His skin seemed to tingle as he passed certain areas and crystal cases in the store, almost causing him to shiver, like a rat crossed over his grave.

Making his way across the shop, Keebo spotted Chelois patiently cleaning the crystal top of the largest counter. Chelois, with her long blonde hair wrapped in a ponytail, was half-elven on her mother's side. She lived here in Stormhaven a few months out of the year, trying to learn an appreciation for her father's trade. The other months she would live in the forest city of Elomir with her mother and her peoples. She had grown into a beautiful young lady, which was quite different from the little girl who always tried to use him as some kind of animated doll. Her father had done business with his mother for many years.

"Um hum," clearing his throat as he tried to gain her attention. She would have had to know he was there, who else would have made the door chime.

Chelois raised her head, seem to peer around the store, and then went about her business.

"Um hum," this time clearing his throat very loudly, causing the girl to smile and let slip a little giggle. "Come on Chelois, has it come to this?"

"Oh Keebs, of course I see you. Still wearing your brother's hand me downs? I would have dressed you so much better," stated Chelois with a playful smile. Looking down at his brother's old shirt, he smiled to himself. If she only knew, he thought to himself. Definitely more to this "doll" than she could imagine.

Keebo pulled his final bundle out, marked with the master jewel crafter's name on it, and pushed it up on the counter. Master Leroit was out of the shop on other tasks, but had left Chelois to assume any duties that would arise while he was gone. Keebo removed the small roll of parchment from underneath the bindings. Unrolling the instructions from his brother, he recited them to Chelois, answering any questions she or her father might have when he returned. Not having any, he placed the directions back in the bundle and bowed deeply to Chelois, causing her to smile and curtsey accordingly. With the sun now far enough to the west that the buildings threw shadows across the streets, Keebo closed the door and headed home to the Green Forest.

CHAPTER TWO

Keebo soared around the flame engulfed spires, as numerous buildings burned below. Spotting the crimson scaled dragon, Keebo soared even higher. Higher than he had ever flown. With great sweeps of his tail, the serpent knocked the bothersome archers from their places on the battlements. Eruptions of flame burned the Watch as they tried to clear the streets and keep order. Keebo's spiked plate armor glistened in the sunlight as a shining star for all to see. Craning its long neck, the dragon glared at the shining star up above. With a horrific roar the dragon flapped it wings, causing winds of nearly catastrophic proportions, lifting its body toward the heavens. The spear that Keebo held shimmered with unimaginable arcane might. Pointing it down toward the puny mortal dragon, Keebo dived down, splitting the sky with a great thunder clap. Like a bolt of lightning he flew toward the dragon. Opening its gaping maw, fire erupted from its gullet, swallowing the metal clad hero. Then as if the gods had sundered the world, Keebo thrust his majestic spear into the beast, bursting forth from its scaled chest, causing it to plummet to the ground below, its gargantuan size crushing numerous buildings. Landing abreast its bloodied carcass, the tiny Hauflin landed, to the cheers of the whole of Stormhaven.

From the dragon's chest, to the street below, Keebo, flapping his own majestic wings, landed, awaiting the prize for his triumphant victory. Waiting for him to remove his shimmering helm, a beautiful Hauflin princess sauntered up to him. Removing his helm, he closed his eyes to receive the well-deserved prize, when it happened. She purred, then licked, then purred again.

Opening his right eye ever so slowly, his Hauflin princess had been replaced by the curious whiskered face of Edwyn's long-haired calico tabby. Grasping the whiskered face of the tabby, he peered into its deep blue green eyes.

"DAMN IT, PATCHES," he wearily sighed. "So

close, so very close."

Reaching a tiny hand up to the tabby's furry head, Keebo scratched between her cupped ears. Purring the happy feline licked his face one more time before it turned and headed toward the small wooden door that was partially open. The bells of the clock tower had barely tolled five times before the cat's interruption, but the wooden carts with squeaky wheels could already be heard moving their wares up and down the dew covered cobblestone streets. Although slightly earlier than usual, he crawled out of bed one foot after the other on the rungs of his small ladder. His brother had left the hearth lit the eve before to help dry numerous bunches of herbs, allowing for the boards of his floor to be warm to the touch. That was one of the benefits to having a bedchamber above the drying room.

Crossing the wooden floor, he reached for the small pitcher full of water. Filling the ceramic wash basin, he slowly splashed water onto his smooth face. He sometimes wished that he had the stubbly growth that his older brother woke up with as he stood rubbing his chin imagining a tuft of hair forming a beard. But Hauflins were not gifted or cursed in that way. Washing thoroughly, he picked out a good patched pair of dark brown breeches. Pulling them on, he then slid his small leather belt through the loops and buckled his shiny brass buckle. Then next to secure his wings and tail he slipped on his small harness, fastening them tightly against his back. Shuffling through a stack of shirts handed down to him from Edwyn, he picked a green Damatron shirt with mid length sleeves, of course that would have to be rolled up for him. Strapping his trusty dagger onto his side, he headed for the hallway and the kitchen below.

Sweet, as well as pungent smells wafted from the kitchen as Keebo made his way down the stairs toward the illuminated backroom. Standing back bent over the table, was Edwyn meticulously reading the pages of a dusty old hide bound tome that had belonged to mother. Finger following every line, as he collected and added numerous ingredients to the boiling pots and flasks. Edwyn seemed very preoccupied. Slowly, stepping over the creaking third step of the stairs, Keebo silently made his way down the stairs and behind his brother. Stepping ever closer, he crept into the kitchen and around two straw-filled crates that had been haphazardly stacked. Holding a small finger to his lips and looking up at Patches, whose curiosity was about to its peak, shushed the feline as if not to alert her master. From stairs to crates, from crates to table he shifted like a shadow. Moving into position behind his prey, he reached out and grabbed Edwyn's leg, causing his older brother to come close to hurtling the table, dropping a spoonful of powdered wormwood into the creases of the tome.

Breathing hard and heart racing, Edwyn tried to gain his composure. Looking down, his eyes found their way to the sight or an innocent looking Hauflin with a grin stretching from ear to tiny ear.

"Morning Edwyn. You look a little jumpy, did I scare you?" the lad stated with a slight grin on his face.

"No, Um not at all, Keebs. I knew you were there all the time," Edwyn said with a little surprise still in his voice. Then he looked at Patches and stated as he scratched her ears. "And thank you for the warning, I see who you like better this morning."

"You're up early this morning, little brother. Not dreaming well?"

"No, the dreaming was great. It was the purring princess. She was the problem." stated Keebo as he climbed up on the stool next to the table and stared at the tabby who was yawning on a stack of parchments.

Fanning the powdered wormwood from the tome's binding, Edwyn gave the younger of the two a peculiar look. "Purring princess?"

"It's a long, long story," the Hauflin sighed. "So

what's on the agenda for today, I see you have risen early this morning as well?"

The truth was Edwyn was always awake by the time Keebo woke up and his brother always went to sleep after the Hauflin on most occasions. Edwyn had never even made time to have his own family he had always just taken care of his younger brother. For an instance a despairing thought crossed Keebo's mind, was he chaining brother to a lonely existence, an existence with only a plump calico tabby to call friend. A plump calico tabby, named Patches that ruined a perfectly grand dream. And as quickly as the sad notion had entered his Hauflin mind, it had been replaced with another flitting moment in time.

"I packed your haversack with some odds and ends to barter in the Burrows. And I would also like for you to make time to stop by the Tallbreeches and check on the lady of the house," stated Edwyn as he handed his little brother a parchment list of small folk specific items. Handing Keebo a small leather purse containing numerous coins, he tried to slide in a short lecture on wisely spending your hard earned coin, which always seemed to cause the Hauflin to get a glazed over look. Keebo knew how to hang on to his coin, it was second nature to him. Out of all the small folk, Hauflins had a talent for holding on to anything, no matter who it belonged to. Jiggling the pouch, taking a mental note of the coins within, he slowly placed it into the folds of his shirt. Pulling the straps of the oversized haversack over his shoulders and grabbing a piece of last eve's leftovers, Keebo left the shop through the door that opened into the alley.

Keebo was met by the sweet scents of jasmine and heartblood as he stepped onto the dew covered cobblestone alley. Most of the shop's rear facing was covered with vines that curled their way around the posts leading to the small balcony garden. Only a few shops had rear entrances leading out into this small alleyway which created a safe and private entry for most of the owners and their carts full of goods.

A warm breeze blew through the maze of streets, slowly evaporating the dew that had settled under his boots. The Green Forest was situated on the western side of the trade district, not far from the gate separating it from the docks. Turning south on The Crooked Path, the lighthearted Hauflin traveled down the busy thoroughfare to the newly created entrance to the ever-expanding Burrows. Passing numerous shops decorated by flower boxes full of blooming blossoms, he greeted with a nod and a smile numerous tradesmen preparing their wares for the day's patrons. The smell of fresh dung mixed with the smells of fresh sweetbreads and pies, as horses pulled carts down the busy street, delivering crate after crate of new goods. Wheels creaked as the clickity clack of horseshoes touched the cobblestones. Dodging around the Biggs, he turned down an alley that had numerous crates and debris strewn about.

Patting a cautious hand on his coin bag, Keebo made his way around the crates toward a small opening in the far eastern wall of the alley. Although as he neared the entrance of the tunnel he didn't see any guards, he could feel the watchful eyes of the Stouts, small folk protectors. Stouts, appointed by the Burrows counsel, guarded and protected all of the public entrances the small folk used to gain entry into Burrows, deterring any Biggs from entering. Walking down the alley, he headed to a stack of crates that seemed to be corralled by a large cargo net. Carefully grabbing the edge of the largest, he tugged until the front of the crate opened to reveal a small carved pathway. Passing through the opening and carefully securing the front of the crate back into position Keebo headed down the slightly sloping pathway, reluctantly named the Run Away Path. The street was named after the brakes failed on a cart full of stones sent workers diving out of the way.

Following the small lamps that hung from the

walls used to illuminate the path, Keebo worked his way past great feats of Dwarven stonework that held the weight of Stormhaven from crushing the small folk below. Every time that he journeyed to the Burrows, this young apothecary seemed slightly bewildered at the immensity of the tiny hidden world. He had grown accustomed to oversized doors, buildings and the Biggs. But here, he was not out of the ordinary, but normal. Somewhat, anyways. Passing numerous Hauflins, Gnomes and dwarfs, who were on their way to work or elsewhere, he made his way to Boater's Way, the main thoroughfare under the Docks. Placing a hand on the corner of the passage way, he peered out in to the tunnel known as the Boater's Way, as small folk of different sizes roamed the street preparing for the day's trade.

Turning north, Keebo made his way up Boater's Way. The smells of the docks above mingled with the Burrows below. Strolling down the street, carts being pulled by sturdy dogs creaked as they made their way with their heavy loads. A nod, a smile or a wave greeted Keebo without the common practice of a patting of the pockets. Young criers took their places on the intersections where other streets diverged. Broadsheets flew from the criers as their crowds gathered, listening for the latest gossip.

"Imp strikes again, Lord makes vow for fair trade with the small folk. Get it here first," yelled a young Hauflin girl with a bundle of broadsheets stuffed under her arm.

"Mouse boy seen near Sparkling Rock! Ten places to hide your cheese," yelled a small Gnomish boy working for the Prancing Pony. "Get prepared now!"

The two criers trying their best to out sale the other, were surrounded as devote readers waited for a chance to grab a broadsheet. Stopping first at the Gnome then the Hauflin, Keebo reached in and, taking a few coppers from the money pouch that was safely tucked within the folds of his shirt, paid for each of the broadsheets. Folding the freshly printed parchments, he slid them into a side pocket on his haversack, which would hold them safe for a relaxing afternoon of perusing. Finally making his way along the curving street, he came upon Hobbler's Junction. Street vendors competed with businesses that occupied the space along the walls. The junction was the trade center of the Burrows, with numerous alleys and cul-de-sacs splintering this more circular shaped intersection. Navigating his way around fierce competitors, Keebo made his way to the tailor's shop. Outside he spotted the tiny wooden sign above the door, embossed with a tiny thimble and a sewing needle. Painted letters spelled out Tallbreeches around the border.

Reaching for the small door handle, carved in the shape of scissors, Keebo peered in the window. The shop was dimly lit by small freely moving orbs of light. But within the shop, dancing with an invisible suitor was a Hauflin girl. As she moved, ribbons and silks seemed to spiral through the air in time with her movements. The world seemed to slow down, no stop, as Keebo watched in awe from the window. He was consumed by her. She was stunningly beautiful and whirled like a petal on the breeze.

"Pretty isn't she, lad? Looks like her mother," a sorrowful voice sounded, bringing Keebo out of his daydream, allowing him to release the breath that he had unintentionally held.

Warmth filled his cheeks as Keebo turned and discovered that Timbles was standing behind him. "G-good day, Master Timbles. I- I was just here to check on your l-lady, sir" stated the surprised Hauflin as the words seemed to stumble from his lips.

Lack of sleep had taken its toll on the small folk tailor. Circles darkened the areas under his eyes which begged for sleep. Leading the boy into the shop, the old man turned and locked the door behind them. Keebo scanned the room, but his eyes seemed to always settle on the petite female that now sat at her sewing table diligently working, not noticing the small ribbons that gently glided silently to the floor. As he crossed the front room of the building, the hairs tingled on the back of his neck. Beautiful cloaks and gowns hung from the walls and free standing racks. Timbles didn't say a word to his daughter as he led the young man past the seamstress, through the red velvet drapes covering the hallway to the other rooms.

Looking back at Keebo, Timbles sighed as he pulled another key from his pocket. Placing it in the key hole and turning the key, pins slid into place unlocking the door. Movement could be heard on the other side of the small wooden door, as the tailor placed the key back in his pocket. With a sigh the old man slowly tugged on the handle, allowing the door to open a crack. Light filtered into the room as the door opened. As the light hit the darkened recesses of the room, Keebo caught the glimpse of a small creature running to and cowering in the corner.

"Sari, darling it's me. It's me, Timbles." The old man said as he slowly entered the room moving toward the creature that huddled in the corner. "You have a guest, Sari. He is here to help you."

Nearly speechless, Keebo watched as tiny clawed fingers reached out and grasped Timbles' out-stretched hand. This couldn't be the Timbles' wife. This didn't even look Hauflin. The old man led the creature back to the bed and after laying it down, pulled the blanket back upon it. Not making any swift movements, the young apothecary removed his haversack and placed it by the wall. Then he moved carefully into the bedchamber and towards the creature lying on the bed. Hairs tingled down his neck and spine as he moved closer to the creature. Timbles softly caressed the creature's head carefully and pushed its hair from its face. Moving to the side of the bed, Keebo peered into the eyes of the creature. Hauflin eyes looked back filled with sorrow and fear. With Timbles help, the young apothecary carefully examined and noted every detail no matter how small. Sari still had a fever, although it had started to diminish. Her hands and feet were slowly drawing up into small claws as coarse hair grew from her skin. Front teeth becoming more pronounced. Ears and facial features had started to elongate into features resembling a, Keebo thought, a rodent. Checking one last thing, the young apothecary listed the beginning of a tail protruding from her tailbone.

As Sari trembled in the arms of her husband, Keebo slowly made his way back to his haversack that lain against the wall. Opening several of the pockets, the young apothecary dug out several items: a long needle, two vials, and a small razor sharp dagger. From behind Keebo, a soft voice consoled the nervous woman with a trembling voice, mixed with the slightest hint of squeaks. Turning around, the young Hauflin, again slowly moved toward the bed, pulling a small chair alongside the woman. Meticulously, the small apothecary produced the dagger and carefully shaved a small area of her arm, collecting a sample of hair. The sight of the dagger caused the poor woman to shudder as a primal fear tried to take hold. Burying her furry rodent muzzle into the shoulder of her husband, her body trembled. Carefully, the hair was placed in the first vial. Next softly taking her hand in his, Keebo stretched one of her tiny clawed fingers out and pierced it with his needle allowing the dark red vitae to drip into a vial that he quickly stoppered. Gently applying pressure, the wound slowly stopped bleeding.

"We will help you, Sari," stated Keebo as he placed a calming hand on her shoulder. Catching Timbles' attention, he gave a small nod toward the door and rose to collect his bundle. Glancing over his shoulder, he eyed Timbles slowly kneeling down and kissing his beloved on her forehead as he whispered something softly and between only them. Leaving the room, with the old tailor in tow,

Keebo headed for the small kitchen that opened directly across from the bedchamber. Sitting down at the table, Keebo took out his notes, splaying them across the small surface. Timbles turned the key in the lock until it clicked, and then walked into the kitchen, taking a seat across from the young Hauflin.

From the small hearth in the corner, a small kettle whistled, allowing the steam to escape. The tailor rose from the table, gathering two tiny tea cups and poured him and his guest some Paddleleaf tea. Keebo graciously accepted the tiny cup and slowly sipped the tea, as the aroma wafted around the room.

"IT DOESN'T MAKE SENSE, SIR," Keebo stated as he poured over his notes. "I need you to tell me everything, from the beginning, of when Sari became ill until now."

Nervously the old man scratched his head where his long hair had begun to thin. "All I know is that one eve, almost a tenday ago, I found her wandering the junction. She seemed disoriented and couldn't remember anything after stopping at the bakers. Her basket was still full of bread. Then the following morn, she started to feel feverish and her spirits were dampened. The healers at the temple couldn't do anything, so I decided to go above to your shop. Your mother had a good reputation, even down here."

"Could she have had a complication while practicing the arcane?"

"What do you mean, the arcane? My poor innocent wife was not one of those damn wizards who locked themselves up in a tower." exclaimed the tailor as an irritated look became more apparent on his face. The old man started to rise to his feet, "How dare you!"

"WHOA, WHOA, WHOA," Keebo exclaimed as he held his hands up trying to calm the older Hauflin. "I didn't mean any disrespect towards your lady. I am just trying to consider all the possibilities."

As the old tailor sat back down, Keebo gathered his notes and drank the last sip of tea, which had started to cool. The young apothecary had felt the hairs tingling on his neck as he had entered the shop and the back room, but there could have been some other reason his senses were becoming active. Following after Timbles, he made his way to the front of the shop where the seamstress once again caught his attention. She let out a small giggle as Keebo absentmindedly ran into a small rack of baubles. Bells and brightly colored buttons fell to the floor, as the young apothecary clumsily tried to catch them. Quite embarrassed, he reached down and grabbed what he could with nervous hands, while trying not to make eye contact with the girl. Feeling her eyes on him, he quickly headed to the door where Timbles waited expectantly, shaking his head.

LEAVING the building and entering into the busy junction, Keebo turned and placed his hand upon the Timbles' shoulder once more. With a heartfelt look, the young apothecary told the tailor that he and his brother would do all that they could to stop the affliction that consumed his love, his soul mate. Then the young Hauflin turned and made his way down Boater's Way toward the Green Forest. Traveling homeward, his mind raced, mentally comparing the details of the visit to the smudged pages of his own leather bound tome. But then his thoughts seemed to drift to the tailor's daughter. She was so beautiful, and he was such a klutz. Kicking a loose stone down the way, the boy kept his eyes down, embarrassed at his clumsiness. It would never work anyway he thought, he was just too different. Consumed by his own thoughts, he reluctantly turned onto the Run Away Path and headed up the sloping corridor to the city above.

CHAPTER THREE

*O*n bended knee, in the cool darkness a lone petitioner kneels before a rune engraved black longsword. Draped over its pommel, a dark silken standard slowly sways in the warm breeze, created by one of the numerous enchantments still active in this private sanctuary. Alone, in silent reverie, the petitioner pays homage to a distant god no longer able to hear his prayers.

Breathing deeply, the petitioner rises to his feet. Standing nearly six feet tall, the figure stretches, allowing his great draconic wings to extend to their full length. Horns spiral toward the ceiling as the petitioner rolls his head around. Bones pop and creak as its stiff joints loosen up. Holding its six fingered hand in the air and making a quick gesture, small wisps of magical fire brighten the dark room. Walking slowly to the small pedestal next to an ornate dark wooden door, the creature carefully dips his hands into an obsidian basin filled with clear water. Cupped fingers catch the water as the infernal-blooded creature brings the cool liquid to his face and over his head, smoothing down long blonde hair streaked with silver. Turning toward a grand mirror, his reflection showed a gem embedded where his left eye once rested. A small grin appears as he uses a piece of midnight blue velveteen cloth to dry his face and hands. Manipulating the tarnished silver serpentine band encircling his index finger, the creature begins to shift into a more appeasing form. Dwarfed now by the dark robes worn by his former form, a silver haired elf removes the garment, only to replace it with the attire of a tradesman. Draping his traveling cloak over his arm, he reached for the ornate obsidian door handle. Opening the door, the silver haired elf stepped through the portal into the hall way of his private quarters occupying one of the various sub-basements of his lucrative business.

The smells of fresh pastries filled the hallway as a woman could be heard singing down the way. Eying the aged portraits as he walked by, the elf made his way down the hall to the origin of the singing. Looking in through the open doorway, he spied a woman whose back was turned away from the opening. Quietly he moved, like a shadow in the night, behind the unsuspecting woman. The elf, pausing only a second as the woman held an enchantingly long note, wrapped his strong arms around her, embracing the woman. Turning her around he noticed that the soft light caused the light blue scales that intermittently covered her body to sparkle. Her surprised look softened into an adoring smile as she embraced him back.

"Morning my love, did I surprise you?" stated the elf as he held her tightly against his chest.

"As always my dear, but a pleasant surprise!" caressing his face leaving flour smudges on his cheek.

Drinking her in with a kiss, he slowly released his embrace. Grabbing a freshly baked biscuit and smothering it with honey, he turned with a smile and headed to the double doors leading to the offices above. Placing his hand on the railing and speaking the words, *Secario Mentalos*, the spiraling staircase extended up until it reached the ground floor of the building above. Step by step he made his way upwards, only momentarily pausing to unlock the door. As soon as he exited the stairs, he was surrounded by the hustle and bustle of children running to and fro.

"Morning boss" seemed the greeting of the day

as different races of children bounded from room to room. In one room, a child pulled on his tabard, proudly displaying the crest of the Darkserpent, the next an older boy handed out letters and packages to be delivered. Smiling at the efficiency at which he could get the orphans and forgotten children of the city to work together he fed them, clothed them and educated them. In exchange, they carried his parcels and kept theirs ears and eyes open. As they grew older or showed great promise, they were even given a chance to join his more lucrative trade of specialty importing and exporting.

The halls hummed with activity, bringing to mind an ant hill. Luckily with the warm weather, the front door could be propped open, allowing for a steady stream of couriers and customers to pass through into the foyer where the office door stood slightly ajar. Peeking in, he could see Filpin carefully arranging ledgers and broadsheets in precise and ordered stacks. Then he moved and opened the window just enough to allow the sounds of the docks to permeate the room, but not enough to allow an ocean breeze to disrupt his neatly stacked pages.

Turning around, the lanky youth snapped to attention as the trades master entered the office. Waiting for his employer to be seated, Filpin opened the first ledger displaying the day's business. Perusing the ledger, the elf ran a finger slowly over the lines, inspecting the accuracy of the young man. Then grabbing the edges, Thucious closed the book and pushed them toward the boy.

"Very good, Filpin," praising the boy. "I wouldn't know what to do without you."

"Thank ya, Boss. Been trying to let some of the young ones run a few more errands than usual, not like break'em in early," said the boy with a smile as he slightly puffed out his chest. "It keeps them busy in the warm weather and almost out of trouble."

"Just keep a good eye on them for me," said Thucious with a cautious look. "If they get into trouble with the Watch, it tarnishes the Darkserpent name."

"Yessum boss, you can count on me," answered the boy as he headed out of the office to receive a new parcel to be delivered.

Flipping through the broadsheets, making mental notes of interesting articles that would need further scrutiny, he settled on a small parchment called the *Prancing Pony*. Half the size of the common broadsheets, the small rolled parchment had made its journey from the Burrows to his desk in the pocket of a gnomish courier. Understanding the language of some of the small folk was hard enough, but trying to comprehend the subtle nuances of the written language was entirely different. Double meanings and secret messages abounded in most of the articles, undecipherable even for some of their most loyal of readers.

Many of the articles either contained birth announcements of an ever growing family or news from the world above. Although most stories presented a hint of exaggeration, Thucious settled on the peculiar headline "Mouse boy seen near Sparkling Rock! Ten places to hide your cheese." A grin appeared on the face of the elf, the imagination of the small folk always seemed to lighten the mood of any dreary day. Reading on, the story seemed to detail a lamplighter's account of being chased by a relatively quick creature seen skulking along the way of Sparkling Rock. The Hauflin out of breath and ducking behind a crate described the creature as being the largest mouse he had ever seen running on two legs. The rest of the column reluctantly contained a list of ten ideas the editor thought were good hiding places to protect your stores of cheese.

Finishing the rest of the tattered broadsheet, Thucious placed the *Prancing Pony* on his desk. Yelling loud enough to penetrate the finished wooden walls, Filpin answered the call with a knock on the office door. Slowly opening the door and peering in to the sunlit office, he entered with a respectful nod.

"Ye boss," answered the lanky youth as he tried to also keep one ear on the front door.

"Filpin, send Tink in here for a moment. I need a Hauflin's interpretation of this broadsheet." Thucious said as he patted the small piece of parchment.

"Sir," hesitated the youth while trying not to make eye contact. "Tink didn't show up again this morning. No one has heard from him."

"What do you mean no one has heard from him?"

"He didn't show this morning again, sir, so I had told Jes to check on him when she was done with her delivery to the northern Burrows."

Jes or Jesapina Twinklebuckles, was a young gnomish girl that had an aptitude for minor illusions, but due to an uncanny knack for being in the wrong place at the wrong time, was rescued from a notoriously boring life in a workhouse created for troubled youth. Thucious, a conduit for the arcane himself, could appreciate her talents and bought her freedom in exchange for her loyalty.

"Send her in as soon as she arrives," said Thucious as a strange feeling of dread inched its way in to his thoughts. Maybe just instinct or just knowing the boy, Thucious' thoughts whirled awaiting news.

As the clock tower tolled one bell past the midday sun, a young flame-haired Gnome bounded down the hall and into the office. A carefree smile stretched across her face as she skipped to musical notes only she could hear. Jumping up on the dark stained wooden chair setting in front of the desk and twirling around, she stopped only to take a long and pretentious bow, before plopping down on the crimson goose down cushion.

"Fare winds boss, heard you needed me?" she said as her head swayed to the same ghostly melody. "What can I help you with?"

Reminding Thucious of a flighty sprite, Jes' outlook on life always seemed to make the world a little brighter. He watched as the young Gnome fidgeted in the chair, for the ability to sit still seem to elude her.

"Did you happen to stop and check on Tink as you finished your business in the Burrows this morning?" Thucious said.

"Well boss, I kinda did," Jes said as she twisted in her chair and examined the walls for any changes. "I stopped by and banged on the door, but Tink didn't answer. I thought I heard someone talking in there, so I tried to look in the window, but the shutters were pulled tight."

Dipping the elaborate feathered quill one last time in the ink well, Thucious scribbled his signature on the parchment in front of him. Taking a second for the ink to dry, he then folded the parchment and sealed it with a dark wax, placing his seal upon it. Putting the letter in a drawer, he then inserted a crude tuning forked shaped key in the lock and turned it until all the tumblers had slid into place.

"I have a feeling we might need to check on our little friend," Thucious said as he pushed his chair back and stood up. Once more twisting the tarnished silver band around his finger, he started to shrink. Out of sight he dwindled, causing Jes to stand with her hands on the desk peering over to watch her boss disappear out of sight. Walking around the back of the desk, a Hauflin man dressed in a set of traveling clothes stared up at the red headed Gnome, whose attention still was concentrated over the desk.

With a loud "Uh hum," the Hauflin cleared his throat, startling the young girl. Looking down, her whimsical smile seemed to broaden as her eyes settled on her boss that was now shorter then she was. Placing hands on her small shapely hips, she cocked her head to one side carefully eying her boss' new persona. Launching herself from the chair, she gracefully landed beside him.

"Always a Hauflin," exclaimed Jes as she tried to portray her best pouting expression. Then with a giggle, her smile crept through. Rising up on his tippy toes, Thucious reached for the door handle, and with a firm pull opened it gaining access to the hallway. With Jes in tow, the two small folk entered the fray as children scrambled down the hallway and into the city abroad. Stepping out the doorway, the day was warm and smelled of the sea. Wagons carried goods as sailors and dockworkers made their way to and from the ships docked in the harbor. Avoiding horses and oxen, the two hurriedly crossed the busy streets, dodging down alleys still lit by the daylight. The Watch made their rounds like clockwork during the day, but at night when the ghostly mists rolled in from the harbor, sometimes even they were scarce. Nearly half a bell toll later, they had made their way from Darkserpent Couriers through the maze of streets to a small alley, whose entrance was situated in an alcove off Whalebone Court.

As they followed the cobblestone covered alley, Thucious noted how masterly strewn stone walls converged, blotting out the sky as the slope of the alleyway slanted down. The two made their way along the path as numerous small folk trudged along to and from there destinations. Following dog drawn carts and numerous types of foot traffic, the alley which had turned into a tunnel opened not far from Hobbler's Junction on Boater's Way. The smell of pipeweed wafted up the corridor from the vendor who had set up shop not far from where the alley exited. Grabbing his hand, Jes pulled Thucious through the busy streets heading north up Boater's Way to the section of the Burrows called the High Burrows, which lay partly underneath the villas of the older noble families. The High Burrows was much younger than the area located underneath the Docks. The small folk nobles, if such a thing had ever existed, lived in there.

From Hobbler's Junction, they turned on Sparkling Rock, following the inclining street into the Burrows. The atmosphere was noticeably different from the section below. Natural sunlight bounced from the streets above by carefully placed mirrors illuminating different sections of the burrows. As Thucious passed several small gaudy decorated shops, he was reminded of the surface upscale business, just smaller in scale. Jes, now with the Hauflin in tow, weaved between small folk, heading deeper into the burrows until they came to a small cul-de-sac containing a group of homes at the end of Sparkling Rock. The homes there were somewhat of an eyesore, tucked away out of view of the rest of the High Burrows.

Common Hauflins and Gnomes made the place home after the earthquake that followed the maelstrom of 1226, which had twisted numerous tunnels in the Burrows.

The street was dim as they made their way to the front door of the small home. Shudders pulled tight, they moved to the door facing the street. Jiggling the handle, the door had apparently been deadlocked from within. Thucious knocked loudly on the door, which was answered with silence. Looking at Jes, he motioned for her to stand back as he pulled the crude tuning forked shape key from his pocket. Striking it against his small hand, the key started to glow as it softly began to hum and vibrate. Moving the humming key next to the keyhole, the vibrations sent rolling waves through the lock. First one tumbler, then another could be heard clicking into place. When no more noise came from the locking mechanism, Thucious tugged lightly on the handle, opening the door.

Cracking the door slightly, the Hauflin slowly peeked into the room beyond. Darkness consumed the room. Leaning toward Jes, Thucious softly whispered in her ear.

"This form doesn't allow me to see in the darkness, I need you to be my eyes," he said.

Leaning in close to the door, Jes scanned the room as a shadow crossed her view. Quickly yanking her head back, she looked at her boss with a concerned look.

"Somethun's in there, boss. It was small but fast, really fast."

Moving her out of the way, Thucious slowly grabbed the edge of the small door, taking a deep breath he thrust the door open, bathing the room in the dim light of the street. The room was in shambles as its sparse furniture laid broken and strewn about the floor. Carefully moving into the room, the two noticed a door partially ajar, leading into what could possibly be Tink's sleeping quarters. Jes drew a small curved dagger and moved toward the door. Incoherent mumbling could be heard coming from the room as a stench of garbage seeped from the opening. Moving his small Hauflin fingers in unison, Thucious called a small globe of light into being and sent it into the room. As the globe entered the room, Thucious grabbed the door handle and pulled it quickly shut. A bright flash of light radiated from the cracks in the door, followed by the unintelligible screams of the creature within. Throwing the door open, the bright flash had reduced to a faint glow. Curled in the corner, a small rodent-like creature cowered, covering its eyes. Around it, the tiny leftovers of numerous meals had been strewn about the floor.

With a burst of speed the tiny creature

exploded toward the two, knocking Thucious down and landing on Jes, taking both of them to the ground. As the creature tried to crawl over her, Thucious grabbed its legs, interrupting his escape. The creature, trying to flee, now wrestled with the master courier pinning him to the ground. Regaining her balance, Jes maneuvered to the two combatants and brought the pommel of her curved dagger down upon the creature's head. With a soft wet thumping sound, the creature's body grew limp and slumped into Thucious' arms. Pushing the thing off his chest and on to the floor, Thucious sat back against the wall, inhaling deep as he tried to catch his breath.

Coarse hair covered the tiny body that lain face down on the floor of the courier's home. Using his boot, Thucious nudged the body on its back. Eyes closed, the creature's chest rose and fell with every breath. Jes, using her dagger, shredded a tattered sheet into strips. Both fell to the task of binding the creature's wrists and ankles. Jes pulled the scraps of cloth tightly, carefully binding its wrists. Moving toward its ankles, Thucious cautiously knelt down to bind its feet. The gnarled feet were covered with scraggy brown fur.

These events seemed peculiar Thucious thought as he pulled the right leg closer to the left. Certain aspects, Tink's disappearance, the ransacked home, the rodent creature's burst of speed, taunted his thoughts. Glancing down to bind the first ankle, he noticed that the fur seem to have a slight reddish hue just barely noticeable. With nimble fingers, he slowly raised the tattered leg of the breeches. At first glance it seemed that a line of red fur snaked its way up its leg, but looking closer it wasn't the fur at all but illuminated skin, a birthmark.

"Ah Tink, what have you got yourself in to?" exclaimed Thucious as he rubbed his own head as all the pieces fell into place.

"What boss, you think this thing killed ol'Tink. I'll wake up the mangy thing, boss and you can make it tell us!" stated Jes as she nudged the rodent with her boot.

"Jes, there's no need," said the Hauflin as a solemn look appeared on his face. "I have a feel'in that this, this is Tink!"

Color seemed to drain from the girl's face as she knelt down beside the creature that now lain bound on the floor. Taking its tiny head in her hands, she turned it until she could see its face. How could this be her friend she thought, her curious compatriot? Then his eyes fluttered open, momentarily, and then closed. But a moment was enough to see her old friend. With a look she asked the same question her mentor had wondered himself. How? Thucious, staring at Tink, sat on the wooden floor collecting his thoughts. Instructing Jes to finish binding his legs, he watched the Gnome's trembling hands slowly tighten the strips.

After they had secured the ratling and moved his unconscious body carefully to the bed, the two searched the abode, to no avail. They just couldn't find anything detailing what had befallen Tinker. Understanding the need to move him to a more secure location, Thucious made plans to transport his tiny friend back home. Handing Jes a small platinum coin stamped with a serpent, he sent her to acquire the services of Drutin, an owner of a wagon with a strong pony, who would ask no questions. Drutin was an old gray dwarf that had retired numerous years ago from smuggling, when necessity required he disappear. Picking a chair up from the floor, he sat by the cursed ward, keeping a watchful eye, and awaited the Gnome's return.

Wheels on cobblestone pulled the Darkserpent from his deepening thoughts. The red headed Gnome slowly opened the front door and cautiously peeked in, scanning the room. Focusing on her boss, the young Gnome did not enter the home until she saw a lone hand wave her in.

"Boss, I found him," whispered Jes as she gave a thumb toward the door. "He was drinking his fill down at *The Pick and Hammer*."

Carefully they rolled the ratling in blankets and maneuvered him to the door. Drutin had backed the small wagon up to the door and removed numerous wooded planks covering the wagon's bed, revealing a hidden compartment. Placing the bundle in the hold, the dwarf and Hauflin quickly secured the boards, hiding quarry from sight. Loading up, the four made their way through the winding passageways to the streets above. Night had fallen in the city above and few wagons traveled after dark. Carefully they made haste through the lamp lit streets of the docks to arrive at the rear entrance of the courier shop. In the shadow of the old warehouse, the wagon pulled next to the tattered unloading dock. Quietly the old dwarf went about his business uncovering the hidden compartment, first removing one board then another. Grabbing the blanket wrapped cargo, Drutin heaved it into the arms of his two other passengers. With a nod to Thucious, the dwarf meticulously placed the boards back in place. Pulling on the reins, the spotted pony pulled the cart down the alley along the cobblestone street.

CHAPTER FOUR

*T*he summer heat radiated from the terracotta shingles of the aged, three story warehouse, keeping the small winged Hauflin warm as night descended on the city. Perched on the stone ledge and overlooking the shadowed streets below, Keebo took his place among the other gargoyles adorning the building. Wrapping his wings and tail close to his body, he watched as the lights of the city began to dot the darkening landscape. Below, with poles strung over their shoulders, lamplighters hurried down the way doing their part to fight back the enveloping darkness.

As the hours passed, counted only by the tolls of the clock tower, the traffic traveling the streets had diminished to the green glow of the Watch's lanterns, as the patrols made their rounds. Intoxicated lovers found their way, staggering into many strange bedchambers, as the lawless melted into the deeper shadows. From his three story advantage point, his view expanded over the smaller buildings to the adjacent streets. The small motionless avenger pulled his dangling legs back onto the ledge and stood to stretch and relieve his aching muscles. Reaching high into the air, he arched his back and extended his arms and wings, stretching them. As he started to exhale a deep breath, he happened to catch a glimpse of a greenish light of a watch patrol illuminating the walls of several buildings as it moved quickly down the street. And then he heard it, the droning blast from a Watchman's horn.

Hearing the horn, Keebo flattened his wings against his back, trying to blend into the shadows covering the ledge. Another horn sounded in the distance, answering the first. This would now be an interesting night thought the Hauflin, as a smile appeared on his lips. The Watch's lights and yells seemed to work in unison as they inherently maneuvered their quarry toward each other, forming a wall of flesh and steel. The sounds of hard soled boots on cobblestone were followed by the orders barked by the young captain, who was trying to catch his breath. Watching from the ledge he noticed that the streetlamp down below seemed to slightly dim, casting a shadow on the alleyway adjacent from the warehouse. The tiny hairs on his neck raised as a tingling sensation arose. Finally, Keebo thought, he would get to see what magic wielding Bigg kept the Watch busy this night. Concentrating on the alleyway, he was surprised when a tiny cloaked figure carrying a bundle over his shoulder stuck its head out of the darkness.

Carefully moving into the street, the tiny vagabond looked both ways before turning and motioning for the other to follow. Slowly, two more small folk appeared from the alley. Hobbling, one of the small folk worked on crossing the street, as the voices and footsteps of the Watch grew closer, descending on their position. Losing its footing, the smaller of the two followers fell to the cobblestone clenching its thigh.

"Go on, I will catch up when I can," a female voice said.

"No, we go together, or we stand and fight. We're not leaving you, Fleur," stated another female, "Bells can darken the street or carry you and I will take the bag. Or, or we can try to hide until they pass."

"Move me over next to those barrels, and take off you two, I will just slow you down, I should have been more careful. We all knew the risks and

I still plan to survive this. The Biggs will pass by and then I will work my way home when I can. Our families need that coin too bad. Now go," stated Fleur with a commanding voice.

Looking at the each other with a shrug, Bells handed his bundle to the larger female. Reaching down, he slowly lifted Fleur to her feet and helped her limp to a space behind some old tattered barrels. Nodding one last time as a sign of respect, Bells quickly took the bundle from the other, and proceeded down the street into another alley with the female in tow. As they turned into the alley, the lamplight seemed to regain its life, illuminating the street once more. The green light of lanterns chased the shadows from the street as the two patrols met at the intersection in front of the warehouse, only feet away from part of their quarry.

"Did you see them, quick little thieves they are," stated the young captain as he removed his helm, allowing his brown locks to surround his face. The other patrol, breathing heavily as well, shook their helmed heads, looking up and down the street. Keebo watched as the small folk remained as still as the stone waterspouts sharing his ledge. Moments later, a strange shriek erupted from the well-traveled street beyond. Shouting out directions, the young captain divided the two patrols again. Taking a deep breath, he adorned his helm and again joined the hunt, trudging down the streets after his foes.

Keebo watched as the commotion at street level subsided and once again everything grew still. His silvery blue eyes became fixed on the tattered barrels that sat undisturbed by the patrols as they passed by. He would follow her he thought, if for no other reason than he seemed intrigued by her. So he waited. One toll of the clock tower, then another. Curiosity seemed to plague him, why didn't she move. Stretching his wings, the Imp leaped into the air and circled the street. It felt good to be in the air once more. Slowly descending, he alighted on the metal lamplight that bathed the street in light. It would soon be morning and the flames would be doused. Carefully keeping an eye on the barrels, he descended again to street level. The cobblestone street would soon be warmed by the morning sun, drying the nightly coating of dew. Slowly making his way to the barrels, he quietly crept to Fleur, keeping one eye on them and the other on the street. His tiny ears didn't detect anything out of the ordinary, but this whole situation wasn't ordinary. Could he have missed her he thought, she couldn't have been able to escape without him noticing. Moving closer to the barrels, his eyes scanned the debris, trying to find any trace of the female. Peering over and around the pieces of broken crates that the largest of the three had leaned against the barrels, Keebo finally noticed the motionless body of the tiny female.

Using his own small hands, Keebo pulled the boards out of the way and examined the female that now lain only partially hidden in the shadows behind the barrels. Clad in black and dark browns, the girl laid wrapped in her cloak, hand still clutching the small dart that had been pulled from her thigh. The tip of the dart oozed with a viscous bluish grey liquid that smelled sweet and intoxicating. He hadn't smelled the poison before, but it would need to be determined later, so he wrapped it carefully before placing it in his satchel. Pulling the hood of the cloak back that covered her face, Keebo stopped and stared at the girl, not realizing that he sat now, with his back against the wall. The tailor's daughter lay before him unconscious from the poison. His heart seemed to skip a beat. Moving her light brown curls from her eyes, the young apothecary noticed that her lips now had started to turn blue instead of the red he had remembered. Removing her gloves, he had discovered that her finger tips as well had a bluish tint. She would need immediate attention before the poison ran its full course. Kneeling down, he carefully placed a nimble hand under her head and started to lift her up, when suddenly, her eyes opened, only momentarily.

"The Imp," she stated in an exhausted voice, as her eyes caught a glimpse of silvery blues eyes behind a harden leather mask, before falling back into unconsciousness. The look in her eyes, the fear, the exasperation, pained Keebo's heart. Straining, he hoisted Fleur into his arms. The tiny veins running through his body seemed to take on an eerie glow. Starting from his little heart to the tip of his fleshy wings, spidery webs of blue arcane energy manifested. Holding her tightly and taking a deep breath, he flapped his wings, lifting them into the air. Higher he soared, as well as his senses, as power surged through every grain of his being. Moonlight reflected off the clock tower as the imp and thief flew over the wall separating the dock and market. Wings flapping in the breeze, the pair headed toward the small window located above the balcony of the Green Forest. Alighting on the small wooden protrusion beneath the small circular window, Keebo gently pushed the window open with his boot. Ducking his head and carefully twisting his body, he and the rogue squeezed through the window on to the wooden beam that stretched across the room. With Fleur in his arms, he cautiously made his way across the beam until it was safe to open his wings and glide to the floor.

Placing her gently on his bed, he proceeded to change out of his leathers and impish mask. As the adrenaline pumping through his veins slowly diminished, so did the arcane energy that coursed throughout his body, allowing his body to lose his glow. Knowing that time was waning, Keebo donned a shirt over his breeches, then proceeded down stairs. Uneasiness gnawed at his stomach, the girl who had stolen his heart may die, but even worse than that she feared him, feared the Imp. Down the hallway he crept, Edwyn would be awake soon enough and Keebo didn't want it to be because of him. Step by step he went until he reached the small kitchen in the rear of the store. Pulling out his mother's book from the cabinet, he hoisted it up on the table. The hide bound tome was heavy and was full of numerous page markers. The boys had always been taught never to get into the business of selling poisons, but always keep remedies to cure them. Looking through the markers, the young apothecary settled on a putrid green colored strip of cloth marking the pages concerning poisons. Natural and concocted, mother had listed them. Removing the dart from his satchel, he started to flip through the pages as quickly as possible, skimming the descriptions.

Page after page he turned until he came upon the picture of a ghoul and a blue looking flower. The title read *"Ghoul's Kiss,"* and proceeded to document a flower collected from the tombs of ancient graveyards. When crushed, the blooms would release a bluish gray liquid that, when boiled, would be reduced to a very sweet and potent poison that would cause the imbiber to take on the resemblance of a corpse, paralyzing the nervous system until a remedy was administered. Running his fingers over the detailed script, the young apothecary finally found what he was looking for. Mid to bottom of the page, the words *"antidote"* stood out in bold letters. One ingredient and only one was listed on the page, powdered horn of the Tagmis. Boiled down and steeped preferably in a tea, but one had to be careful not to drown the afflicted. The other was more direct yet slightly more painful. One could pierce the skin, allowing the mixture to come in direct contact with the blood. Keebo didn't particularly like that method, but drowning the thief seemed to bother him as well. Climbing down to the floor he made his way over to the vine covered ornate cabinet. Unlatching the hand carved ivory latch, he reached in and grabbed a small tube containing ground Tagmis horn. Placing a small amount in a flask, he proceeded to add just enough water to boil the concoction over the small flame they sometimes used as a burner. The powdered horn slowly dissolved, causing the water to slightly turn a dark crème color. Boiling down the mixture, it soon began to thicken into a paste, in which the small apothecary would then administer to the unconscious thief.

The young apothecary returned up the stairs with his antidote in hand. Making his way down the hallway, he met Patches who went out of her way to brush up against him, making one of her nightly patrols keeping the store safe from mice. Placing a hand on the pint-sized latch, Keebo opened his door and entered his room. Carefully he climbed up the ladder to his bed where Fleur lain paralyzed and skin colored by death. Removing her leathers, the young apothecary took every care that a physician would take with a patient. Her extremities had stiffened and her breath had become almost undetectable. Examining her thigh, the poison had shown signs that it had spread throughout her bloodstream, forming spider web like patterns radiating from the festering puncture wound. Filling the hollow portion of a porcupine needle with the salve, Keebo administered the antidote by plunging the needle into the wound caused previously by the dart. The poison seemed to react immediately to the Tagmis horn. The purplish gray webbing that had spread across her body slowly withdrew, concentrating itself around the puncture wound that lightly dribbled blood from the opening. Taking another heaping amount of salve, the young apothecary carefully created a poultice and secured it meticulously with strips of cloth, bandaging the young rogue's thigh. Her eyes fluttered beneath closed lids as the color returned to her cheeks. Tucking her in under the rabbit fur blanket covering the bed, the young apothecary climbed down reluctantly, smiling at the job he had done. Taking a well-deserved rest, he sat in the small wicker chair next to the bed, tilting it back just enough to rest his head against the wall.

A STRANGE FEELING of drifting over the city filled Fleur's mind as she laid feverish in her sleep. Pain radiated from her thigh, causing her to sit up, clutching the wound. Her surroundings were unfamiliar and the room was slightly spinning, causing her to close her eyes. Try to calm down she kept telling herself, as bile rose in her throat. Rubbing her neatly bandaged leg, she opened her eyes, but slowly this time. The room still tried to spin, but concentrating on her breathing, it finally found its resting spot. Peering over the bed railing, she saw that a Hauflin sat resting against the wall next to her leathers and numerous bloody pieces of cloth. He snored softly, balancing on the tilted wooden chair. Sitting in the bed, Fleur tried to recall the fragmented events from the past evening. Rubbing her forehead, she pieced together what patchy memories she could. She remembered the warehouse, being chased by the Watch, and telling Bells and Rosie to leave her, but the rest was sketchy. How she had arrived here was still a mystery, and the other Hauflin, so familiar. Then the vertigo came back with an unrelenting force, causing her to lie back once more or let the bile continue to rise.

Asleep, her unconscious mind still worked on piecing the fragmented memories back together. She was surrounded by the impeding darkness of the alley, her limbs stiffening from the poison that had started to spread through her tiny body. The sounds of the Watch as they moved away from her hiding place. Blood trickled from the small puncture wound warming her thigh. The creature staring down at her, its face contorted from agonies found only in the depths of the Nine Hells, but its eyes seemed different, almost betraying. It reaches down and gently picks her up but doesn't say a word. Great wings spread as it lifts her into the sky, far above the city streets. From her angle she watches as the streets and buildings pass by under them. Fear grips her as she realizes that she has lost control. Was this the end, her deeds judged, she thought to herself. But then her memories fragment again, the imp was replaced by the small sleeping Hauflin. He was removing her leathers and diligently trying to help her. Another sharp pain shot through her thigh and then the Hauflin cut strips of cloth, binding her wound. Her dreams settled as if they were the venom being drawn from her veins.

Drenched in sweat, Fleur opened her eyes, as her fever had broken. Rolling to her side she cautiously looked over the railing of the bed, surprised that the snoring Hauflin had been replaced by her leathers draped over the chair and a crude pair of crutches. Placing one foot then the other on the small but sturdy ladder, she proceeded to climb down to the floor. Weakened by the puncture wound, her leg would not bear her full weight. Limping to the chair, the young rogue sat down and donned her leathers. She scanned the room, looking for a clue of her location. Slipping into her boots a noise, at the door startled her. Standing up, she tried to balance on her good leg, as she raised the other crutch in preparation to defend herself. Watching the door, she awaited her captures.

The handle of the door slowly rose, allowing for it to swing open. Fleur's heart beat in anticipation like the wings of a hummingbird. Keeping her balance taxed her strength, as pain from the dart wound caused her leg to throb endlessly. Slowly the door opened, but instead of an armed assailant she recognized the face of the Hauflin who sat at one time next to her bed.

"I see you are feeling better, but I don't think you will need to use that," stated the Hauflin as he eyed the crutch that had been raised to strike him. Walking through the doorway, he turned and slowly shut the door letting the latch click. "I just thought I would come to check on you."

Fleur allowed the crutch to lower as she examined the Hauflin, who was wearing an apron stained with numerous smudges. "You look familiar," stated the young rogue as she still tried to maintain her balance. "Do we know each other? My mind is a bit foggy."

Keebo carefully moved a little closer, still apprehensive of the crutch now turned club. "We sort of met once, I-I visited your shop to help your mother the other day,"

"The other day, you are the apothecary. I remember now. But how did I get here, where ever here is?" stated Fleur as she rubbed her temples.

"You shouldn't be on your feet, will you not

please sit down? I will try to explain what I know. You are safe here in the Green Forest!" stated the young apothecary.

Keebo watched as Fleur cautiously sat back down, always keeping at least one hand on a crutch. Pulling up a stool, he sat down across from her an explained everything he knew of the night before, well everything an apothecary would know. He told her how she had arrived to his shop, escorted by a friend who had found her lying in the street. He explained that she had been poisoned by the dart he had removed from her thigh and that he was able to counteract its effects. She was in pretty bad shape, but he did what he could to keep her alive, and now she seemed to be doing better.

Fleur had numerous questions, but Keebo paid close attention not to stumble over his answers. They mostly seem to surround the strange friend for whom she would like to pay her respects for saving her. When down deep he knew it was more curiosity than anything. That was the Hauflin way and being a Hauflin himself, he could not fault her for that. All he would tell her was that an acquaintance of his brought her here in a time of need. But then he started asking his own questions about her escapades that brought her to this point, but she talked in as many circles as he did.

"Well I really need to be on my way," stated

Fleur as she could not get the answers she truly desired. "I appreciate your help, what do I owe you?"

Owe me thought the young apothecary he hadn't even thought that she would be indebted to him for anything. "Owe me," stated the apothecary whose nerves finally decided to arrive. "I would like to accompany you home. It is a fare walk to your father's shop and you shouldn't make the trip alone since you should still be resting not walking. Will this be acceptable?"

Fleur eyed him carefully, trying to discern what ruse the apothecary was trying to hide. Although having found none, she reluctantly shrugged her shoulders and agreed. Using a crutch and the back of the wooden chair, she slowly rose to her feet, as pain shot through her thigh.

"Good then, we will go downstairs and I will finish my work while you rest down there. And then I will take you home," smiled the apothecary as he pushed back his stool and opened the door.

"Wait a second, you said you would walk me home?" stated Fleur with a hint of anger.

"I did say I would escort you home. I didn't say when. You need to rest that leg a while, or-or you might lose it!" exaggerated Keebo. "I will escort you home before the eve, I give you my word.

"I don't think," stated Fleur as Keebo raised his hand not hearing anymore.

"We had an agreement!" stated Keebo he stepped back from the doorway, allowing the angry female to limp past him. Pulling the door shut behind them, a tiny smile appeared on his face. He led her to the stairwell and helped her slowly down to the lower floor. The smells of numerous dry herbs and ointments emanated from the floor below. Following the curved staircase, the two Hauflins made their way into the storage room. As they passed by the table, Keebo reached up and grabbed a small dish containing a sweet roll and a piece of fried pork that had been left from breakfast. Pulling back the green curtains that covered the doorway leading to the front of the shop, he led Fleur to the stool behind the counter. She was still quite upset, but after a few attempts to climb up on the stool herself, she reluctantly allowed Keebo to help her.

"Welcome to the Green Forest, Fleur. I will do my best to hurry but I need to help my brother with the shop while it is busy. Please enjoy the food, the rolls are quite good. They were made by the young widow who owns the bakery next door," stated Keebo, "she is sweet on my brother Edwyn."

Turning around, the young apothecary spied Edwyn talking to a silver haired elf that owned a profitable establishment in the docks. Keebo noticed that they seemed to be in a deep conversation as Edwyn thumbed through his leather bound tome, making mental notes of everything the elf told him. Then the elf casually slipped Edwyn something, in which he promptly placed in his pocket. This caused the curiosity to stir within the young apothecary.

"Morning Master Thucious," stated Keebo, as he walked up to the two gentlemen, interrupting their conversation. "How are the docks today?"

"Young Master Keebo," the elf stated with a small bow. "I see you are well, making your mother proud. You and your brother honor her greatly."

"Well Edwyn, if you will investigate that for me I would greatly appreciate," stated Thucious as he turned back to the older brother of the two. "Let me know if you need anything." With a quick nod of his head, the elf made his way through the bundles of herbs and out the front door.

"What was that about Edwyn?" asked Keebo with an interested look. Master Thucious hadn't been in the shop for a long time.

"I will explain later, but for now we need to get today's chores finished," stated Edwyn.

"Later, but he gave" started to state the Hauflin before he was interrupted.

"Later, for now we have work to do. And by the

way are you going to introduce me to your friend, who is special enough to you that you would use Tagmis horn on her?" interrupted Edwyn, whose detailed memory had noticed the vial had been moved.

"She is just a friend, brother. She ran into some trouble last night and ended up here," explained Keebo, "that's all."

"That must have been some trouble for you to save her from a kiss like that," smiled Edwyn at his little brother.

"A kiss, how did you," said Keebo as he realized he had left the book open to the page, "yes brother, quite a kiss.

With an understanding smile Edwyn placed his hand on his brother's small shoulder and proceeded toward the famished female who was finishing her meal. With a bow, Edwyn introduced himself. The young apothecary noticed that her cheeks became flushed as she tried to swallow the large bite of roll in a ladylike fashion. Edwyn told her that he hoped his very capable little brother had treated her well, before he left her to continue his own duties.

As Fleur fidgeted on the stool trying to finish her breakfast, Keebo climbed the small ladder and crossed numerous rafters, collecting bundles that hung from the ceiling. Fleur was amazed at the grace in which the tiny apothecary moved across the beams with no fear of falling. Jumping from beam to beam he collected numerous herbs, placing some in the pockets of his apron and the others he would toss down to the Bigg he called brother. She feared heights, or maybe it was just the fear of falling. But she had never seen a Hauflin so at home moving across the beams, in actuality it kind of amazed her. She seemed entranced by his show of acrobatics, so much so that she had not noticed that Edwyn watched her and him and just smiled. Marking off the last ingredient on the list, Keebo yelled to Edwyn before descending from the rafters. Crossing the beam to the stairwell, Keebo bounded into the storage room and emptied his pockets onto the table in small piles keeping all of the ingredients separated. Replacing his apron for his haversack, he exited the backroom to where Fleur was seated.

"Ready Fleur?" asked the nimble acrobat as he exited from behind the dark green curtain and extended a small hand to help her from the stool.

Looking at the beams that spanned across the ceiling, then back to the Hauflin, a peculiar expression crossed her face. How could an apothecary, no this apothecary, be so nimble so agile? So many questions seemed to swirl in her mind until she finally realized that her escort had extended his hand to her again.

"Uh yea," she answered, her senses returning. Reaching down she accepted his hand and allowed him to help her down to the floor. Testing her leg, she slowly extended it. The wound had healed considerably, thanks to the salve that had been applied to it. Her leg still seemed a little stiff and didn't fully hold her weight, but at the rate it was healing would be nothing more than a small scar within the tenday. Keebo bid his brother farewell as he opened the door for Fleur.

The sunlight warmed the cobblestone street as the two Hauflins casually made their way to the Run Away Path. A salty breeze blew off the great ocean to the west, allowing the great city to breathe a little easier. Keeping a watchful eye on the street traffic, Keebo carefully maneuvered his limping companion through the hazards of traveling the city. Although the jaunt to the Burrows normally didn't take very long, Fleur's wounded leg slowed their pace considerably, which allowed her the opportunity to ask the young apothecary numerous questions.

"So why do you refer to the Bigg as your big brother?" asked Fleur. "You definitely aren't family."

"Simply" answered Keebo as he eyed the tall buildings along the street, "I do because he is."

"He is? That doesn't make sense. You couldn't have had the same mother. Where is your family?" questioned the rogue as she sat sharing a crate, trying to catch her breath.

Staring down the street toward the bay, Keebo watched as a ship sailed from the harbor toward the horizon. Letting out a deep breath as the ship sailed farther out to sea, he started to open up about his past.

"Edwyn has been my brother as long as I can remember, the only mother I have known has been his," stated the Hauflin still watching the bay. "My mother always told me that I was special, as most mothers do. She loved me and cared for me. And she taught me well. My brother has always watched out for me and protected me."

"But where is your real mother?" asked Fleur again as she stared into the distance, trying to see what kept his attention. "Your Hauflin mother!"

"I only have a feeling of my real mother, a touch really, but I don't know her or what she was like. I never did. Neelia raised me, and in my eyes was the only mother I ever had."

Seeing that this was a subject that caused Keebo to withdraw from her, she quickly tucked this set of questions away in her mind and moved on to more appealing inquisitions, as she scooted off the crate and adjusted her crutches.

"So you're pretty brave walking across the beams at the shop, not scared of falling are ya," stated Fleur with a smile, trying to draw him back to the conversation. "I would have fallen myself."

Puffing out his chest a little, Keebo looked at Fleur as he stated "Afraid of falling, nah, it's not that high. I kind of like heights. Like soaring through the skies, now that would be fun."

A whimsical look crossed Fleur's face. "A small folk flying through the air, now wouldn't that be a sight. Next thing you'll want to do is sprout wings like a bird."

Hearing that, the young apothecary was nearly run over by a Bigg carrying a bundle of fishing nets when he absentmindedly stopped in front of him. The stocky dockworker growled as Keebo dodged a kick from his heavy leather boot. With an apologetic nod to the worker, the Hauflin quickly caught up to the other as she hobbled down the street. The questions never dwindled as they reached the Run Away Path. The two exchanged numerous questions during their conversations, and although some answers seemed guarded, others flowed freely like water.

The two young Hauflins visited as they made their way down into the burrows to Fleur's father's shop. Looking at his companion, he was amazed at how at ease she felt in the cramped tunnels of the Burrows, but she had lived there her whole life. It was a nice place to visit, but he definitely preferred the open sky above his head. The rogue explained to the apothecary how life was in the Burrows. They traveled up Boater's Way to Hobbler's Junction. Keebo could tell that Fleur's leg had started bothering her. Motioning her over to a small group of tables, they took a seat, allowing her to rest her leg. Waving to the young wench cleaning the table, Keebo ordered two half-pints of ale and a serving of stuffed sausage on bread. When the food arrived he gladly handed the serving girl a piece of silver, receiving a large smile and a wink in return, which grabbed Fleur's attention.

"Humph" exasperated Fleur as she rolled her eyes at the wench. "I see you have a friend!" She didn't know why it bothered her so much, but it just did.

"Ahh Fleur, I don't even know her. Anyways she's not my, my. Well just not for me," said the apothecary as he could feel the stammering in his voice.

There was a short silence that seemed to last an eternity between them. Keebo hoped that he had not hurt any chances of getting to know the seamstress better. Fleur hoped that she could understand why the wink and smile of a wench would make her jealous towards of all people, the apothecary. With a quick glance they both gulped down the last sips from their half-pints and rose from the table. Keebo took his place at her side as they made the final leg to the tailor's shop. Business was flourishing as they entered Hobbler's Junction. Weaving around the carts of the street vendors they found themselves outside of Tallbreeches.

"I can make it from here, Keebo," stated Fleur as she hobbled up the stairs. "I appreciate the escort."

"You sure you can make it? Your father is probably worried, I can," Keebo started to say when he was interrupted.

"No, no I will be just fine." Fleur said as she placed her hand on the door.

"Okay then, but let me know if you need anything, or you have any problems. With your leg," said the young Hauflin as he turned to leave. Shaking his head and looking at the street in front of him, he bolstered his courage and turned back around. "Fleur can I call on you some time, I quite enjoyed your company," he blurted out before the fear overcame him.

Watching as her hand dropped from the door

handle, his heart was seized by fear. What did he just do he thought to himself. Did I just say that out loud? Fleur slowly turned around, balancing on her crutches, and looked down from the steps at the apothecary. A look of disbelief crossed her face, which soon was replaced by a devilish grin, which seemed to scare him even more. Color leaked from his face as a cold sweat ran down his back. Why did this rogue, this girl terrify him so. He was the Imp after all.

The wait seemed to last forever and just about the time the anticipation grew overwhelming, her devilish grin softened.

"I think that would be a wonderful idea," she said with a smile. Then she turned and left the petrified apothecary amongst the street vendors of Hobbler's Junction.

CHAPTER FIVE

The sun's evening light filtered through smoke wafting up from the beeswax candles, lighting the storage room. With the sign turned on the shop window and the wooden door locked, the older apothecary retired to the task of testing and identifying the affliction that seemed to elude him. Numerous flasks and vials sat around on the table as Edwyn combed through the pages of his mother's hide bound tome. He rubbed his bearded chin as he contemplated the mysterious plight that had affected at least two Hauflins of this great city. Looking down, he had just enough blood left in the vial provided by the Darkserpent for one more try. Walking over to an ornate bookshelf, he slowly reached for an etched silver bowl that depicted the goddess of the moon flying through the night sky. Setting down at the table, he once again started to identify the affliction. Carefully, he slowly poured the contents of the vial into the bowl. As each drop splattered into the silver clad basin, the sound of sizzling erupted from the surface. Examining the droplets, Edwyn watched as the blood seemed to boil and hiss as it touched the surface of the bowl. How could he have missed this, he thought after reviewing his list of symptoms, but something still didn't add up.

Turning through the hand written pages of the tome, he settled on a small divided area decorated with the different phases of the moon. Page after page he read while studying the drawings of numerous creatures. Looking through the passages, he noticed that every entry, listed in their descriptions an exert mentioning the effects of the moon on the afflicted. But as far as he could discern, neither of the Hauflins' conditions revolved around a lunar cycle. In deep contemplation, he barely noticed that his small brother had entered the shop and stepped through the green curtain dividing the rooms.

"What has you so intrigued brother?" said Keebo as he hung his knapsack on the peg next to his apron.

"Just trying to answer some questions about a

patron, but for every answer there seems to be twice as many questions," answered his brother as he studied the descriptions in the tome.

Climbing up onto the stool next to his brother, the small apothecary peered over at the pages that his brother intently perused. The vellum sheets bound in the tome contained drawings of several wolves, bears, tigers and rats that had many human qualities. Many of the pictures also depicted their anatomy and skeletal structures throughout their transformation. As Edwyn flipped through the pages, a particular drawing caught Keebo's eye.

"Edwyn," said the younger of the two as he tapped the page in the book, "What type of creature is that?"

Looking at the drawing Edwyn replied "that is a wererat, an afflicted person that takes the appearance of a rat. Why do you ask?"

"It looks almost like Timbles' wife, but she seemed a little different. That creature has an evil gleam in its eye, she was terrified."

"Are you sure, brother? This is very important, I need you to be sure," stated Edwyn with a concerned look on his face.

"I am positive, but what does it mean?" he declared. How could she be one of those evil creatures, he thought to himself and what about Fleur?

Edwyn mentally compared the description to the list of ailments that had been relayed to him. The details seemed to coincide almost exactly, except for the entries concerning the moon and personality traits. Reading the notations, the apothecary searched for any remedies that could be created from his stores of ingredients. Turning to his younger brother, he told him to gather the ingredients as he read them off. Monkshood and wolfsbane were easily gathered, but the last ingredient seemed unusual. Water blessed by the moon, was an item that had Edwyn wondering. He would have to research that, but maybe he could render the antidote with holy water instead to counteract the creature's natural affinity to evil.

Meticulously Edwyn ground the poisonous blue flowers of the dried wolfsbane and monkshood into a fine powder. As he used the pestle to crush the beautiful flowers, he thought to himself about the ironic tendencies in nature where beauty was often deadly. Pouring the powder from the mortar into a small piece of cheese cloth, he then steeped the mixture in the holy water that sat in a silver chalice, which now seemed to be licked by the blue flames as the concoction boiled.

At the moment the froth of the mixture tried to

escape over the sides of the chalice, Edwyn quickly used a pair of tongs and removed it from the flames. Carefully he funneled the newly made elixir into a vial and sealed it with a stopper coated in wax. Looking over at his younger brother, who was engrossed within the tome's text, he explained that he needed to speak with the Darkserpent on this matter immediately. Placing the vial in his leather satchel next to his traveling tome, he closed the clasp that resembled the blossom of the witch's heartblood which grew along the rear balcony. Tying his traveling cloak and hanging his satchel over his shoulder, he left through the rear door and down the enclosed alley.

THE EVENING WAS STILL warm from the Belfaust's sun that beat down heating the cobblestone streets during the day. This was Edwyn's second favorite time of the year. The blooming of spring's flowers was his first. He didn't get to leave the Green Forest very much during the day which was very apparent from the condition of the patched shirt he wore. But wealth or his appearance to others didn't seem to consume him like it did so many others and although in a hurry to speak to the Darkserpent, he always found the time to stop and smell the flowers along the street. Passing through the gates, Edwyn nodded to the watchmen who were stationed there and proceeded to follow the Downwater down into the docks.

The salty air permeated the whole area. The small breeze blowing in from the sea carried the tunes from the inns and taverns where bards weaved their tales. Sailors and dockworkers roamed the streets searching for drink and wench to quench the thirsts of a hard day's labor. The docks were known to be quite rowdy this time of year as ships from around the realms brought their cargo to the city. The apothecary continually patted his satchel as if that would ward him against the bad elements which lay hidden in the darkened alleyways. Following Downwater Street, Edwyn found himself staring up at the courier shop's painted wooden sign. The Darkserpent's coat of arms was prominently emblazoned on the painted wooden sign of the three story warehouse. Climbing the steps to the front door, he noticed that a lanky youth sat at the front counter diligently writing in a ledger that was almost as thick as his mother's tome.

Grasping the brass ring hanging from a uniquely carved pewter serpent, the apothecary proceeded to gain the attention of the lanky youth at the counter. One knock, then another finally caught the boy's attention. Adjusting his spectacles, he marked his page and closed the ledger. Walking slowly towards the door, the young man cautiously looked out the window and examined the apothecary.

"Can I help you, sir?" asked the boy still eyeing the gentleman outside the door.

"I am here to speak of important matters with the master of this establishment. I am here to speak to the Darkserpent on urgent business!" exclaimed Edwyn trying to mold his kind features into a scowl.

"My boss has retired for the evening, good sir. You will need to return on the morrow or tell me your urgent business, and I will deliver your conundrum to the boss."

Edwyn argued with the boy for several moments before he realized that it had turned into a futile attempt. "Tell your master that I have information on his rodent problem."

Turning away from the door, Edwyn proceeded to exit the stairs and return to the Green Forest when the sound of the door creaking caught his attention. Swirling around, his eyes focused on a silver haired elf standing in the doorway, beckoning him in.

. . .

"WELCOME MASTER APOTHECARY, I hear you have some information for me?"

"Yes, sir," stated the apothecary, "but what I have discovered doesn't make a lot of sense to me. Some of the details just don't add up."

"In my lifetime I have seen many things that didn't make sense to me, but maybe we can sort them out together. Two heads are better than one, on some occasions," Thucious said as flashes of an old battle with a most ill-tempered hydra passed through his mind. "Come now, let us retire to a less public place as not to gain the attention of the curious."

Edwyn followed the silver haired elf through the door past the lanky youth, and traveled down the hallway past numerous doors that had been closed for the evening. The sounds of children could sometimes be heard as footsteps bounded across the floor above. The apothecary remembered visiting this place on occasion with his mother when there would be need of treating a child that had took up residency here. How the years had passed, Edwyn thought to himself. As they neared the door at the end of the hall, Thucious abruptly turned and faced the apothecary.

"Edwyn of the Green Forest," stated the silver haired elf as he locked arms with the man before him. "I will grant you an honor among few, but with this gift a stern price. Swear as your mother did before, on pain of death and friendship that you will never speak to any soul on what you are about to see, about to hear! What say ye?"

The apothecary stood momentarily speechless as the elf's eyes seemed to pierce his soul. He remembered the stories of dark pacts made in the docks, but he trusted Thucious just as his mother had. He had always helped them when they had needed it. Bolstering his courage, Edwyn stared into the elf's eyes and said "I swear it, on pain of death and friendship until the end." Edwyn had never made a pact with anyone except Keebs, but this time it just seemed to be the right thing.

Thucious' eyes momentarily glowed with a hue of blood as power leeched into Edwyn's arm. A crimson light flowed through the apothecary's veins causing small runes to appear momentarily around his wrist and forearm. An eternal contract formed from magic and blood. Then the elf loosened his grip and with a smile turned to grasp the door handle.

The two passed through the door into a large spiraling stairwell. Still mesmerized by the runes that had started to dissipate, Edwyn barely noticed when Thucious touched the railing that he muttered something in a low tone. Arcane symbols appeared along the steps and railing as the stairwell elongated deeper into the floor below. He followed the elf down past the basement of the warehouse to the sub-levels were he had felt, if only momentarily, a sense of vertigo. Stepping off onto the first landing, the two stood before grand double doors carved with motifs resembling the Witch's Heartblood. The designs were seamless as if the motifs had grown from the wood itself. As they moved closer to the doors, protective runes appeared on the frame of the door, which corresponded with the runes that appeared to be running down his forearm.

Placing a solemn hand upon the door, Thucious spoke the words to invoke its enchantments. The wooden blossoms closed as the vines receded from the opening. Grabbing the handle, the elf pushed the doors open, allowing for the sweet smells of the haven to waft into the stairwell.

"Welcome, Edwyn, to my abode." said Thucious as he graciously bowed, allowing the apothecary to enter.

The hallways in which they walked contained numerous aged portraits and beautiful sculptures. The sounds of laughter and glasses clinging bounded down the hall.

"You must forgive me, we had just settled for a late supper when you arrived," stated the old elf.

"We could always set another place, if you are hungry?"

"Master Thucious, I would much like to confer with you about what I have discovered. I do appreciate your hospitality, but this might not wait."

Giving the apothecary a concerned look, Thucious led him away from the main hallway and into the study. The walls of the study were covered with numerous maps of distant lands. Centered behind a large wooden desk, a large portrait hung. The life-size portrait portrayed an odd collection of adventurers, a dark elf, a tinier than normal Hauflin, a centaur female, a half-dragon bard, a blue skinned holy man, and a demon. A small brass plaque beneath only displayed the words "In honorem".

Edwyn settled in the chair across from Thucious and started to discuss in detail his attempts to discern the cause of the infected blood. The apothecary explained step by step of his attempts to find a cure. The elf listened intently, nodding at certain details and making mental notes of the others.

"And then I poured a few drops in to an old silver basin, and it started to sizzle," stated Edwyn.

"Started to sizzle?" said Thucious as this detail perked his interest. "What do you mean sizzle?"

"I mean exactly that. When the blood touched the basin it started to smolder and sizzle." stated Edwyn. "That was when the other details seemed to start making more sense, or maybe less."

"Are you saying that we're dealing with some cursed infectious creature, some type of therianthropic creature." A look of disgust now crossing the elf's fine features, Thucious had long had a problem with lycanthropes.

"Master Thucious, all I am saying is that in both cases I," stated Edwyn before he was abruptly cut short.

"Both cases, what do you mean both cases? How many of the inflicted have you encountered?" asked the elf whose features had grown a little darker.

"Two total, but sir listen to me. The problem is" said Edwyn as he paused to collect his thoughts, "they don't seem to follow the moon's phases. And that is what has caused me a dilemma. I need to examine them in person, but so far I have only your and my brother's information to base my assumptions on."

Pushing back his chair, Thucious headed past the apothecary to the door. Grasping the handle, he firmly jerked it open and stepped into the hallway. With a reverberating yell, he summoned two of his sons, Samuel and Felixacis, to his aid. Upon their arrival he gave them orders to oblige him and his guest. Pointing down the hall, the two young men bounded with the orders of their father.

Turning to the apothecary he stated "let us go and find more answers. I pray you are wrong this time, Edwyn. I pray you are wrong."

Again the apothecary was led down numerous hallways to a small set of guestrooms. Outside one particular room, Thucious' sons stood on either side of the door. Moving his fingers in arcane gestures, he touched each of them in turn, causing their skin to harden like marble, stating it was only a precaution.

"Remain here lads, unless I call for you," directed Thucious as he produced a key and unlocked the door.

As he opened the door, the smell of rotten food wafted through the air, nauseating Samuel, Thucious' human son, turning him green. The smell was appalling. Inside, the contents of the room had been turned upside down. In the corner, a small furry creature peered from under a blanket, tiny whiskers twitching in the air. Thucious turned to the apothecary and motioned for him to stay back while he attempted to corral the creature. The small ratling could be extremely quick at times.

"Tink my friend, I have someone who would like to see you." stated Thucious as he drew closer to the creature. Tink's eyes darted from the elf to the human, then back to the elf. Slowly with an out stretched hand, Thucious gracefully made his way toward the nervous ratling. Then within the span of a heartbeat, the ratling threw back the blanket and proceeded to sprint, with unnatural speed, across the room past the out stretched hand. With a quick grab, the elf tried to get his fingers on the ratling as it shot by him, but only managed to grasp a few small coarse hairs.

"Damn" sighed Thucious. "This will take too long."

Edwyn watched as his host chanted phrases from some forgotten tongue. As he chanted, the apothecary noticed that the elf's shadow elongated toward the ratling, who was trying to climb the opposite wall. The shadow seemed to wrap itself around the infected, seemed to bind it. The shadow magic pulsed with every heartbeat of its creator. Edwyn stared at Thucious, whom manipulated the aberration, had seized the Hauflin and held him a small distance above the wooden floor. Walking toward the ratling, Thucious stretched out a hand. Placing a finger to Tink's forehead, the ratling slowly closed his eyes into a peaceful slumber. Catching the sleeping creature in his arms, the shadowy manifestation slowly shrank back into its normal form.

"I was hoping it wouldn't have come to this, but he is quite quick and I couldn't have him hurting anyone or himself." explained Thucious as he lowered the creature onto a small bed that was in the room. "He will be out for a while, you may examine him now."

The apothecary placed his worn leather satchel on the floor, before kneeling over the sleeping creature. Taking out a small bound tome of parchment, Edwyn meticulously noted every detail he could about the Hauflin's condition. Taking a small silver needle, the apothecary first touched the skin of the ratling, but nothing happened. No sizzle, no burn, no scarring. Then Edwyn pierced the ratling's skin to the point of drawing blood. Looking at the needle, the blood that had covered it began to smolder. Looking back at Thucious, the apothecary rubbed his head.

"I don't think he is inflicted with what I thought, or at least not how we thought. I think there is something amiss here." stated Edwyn with a look of concern.

"Is he or isn't he?" questioned Thucious as he looked at the ratling.

"That's just it, his skin should have of at least blistered when I tested it, but it didn't. It was only when I touched his blood that the taint presented itself."

The two discussed numerous ideas on how Tink had been afflicted, but the answers seemed to conclude with more questions. Edwyn explained that he had tried to distill an elixir based off his mother's notes, but some of the ingredients had to be substituted and he could not guarantee the results or if the Hauflin would survive after using it. Deep in thought, Thucious wrestled with the possible outcomes of using the potion or not. He had decided. Life as this creature was not worth living and he would not allow his friend to endure it.

"Administer it!" stated Thucious as he placed a hand on the bed supporting the Hauflin.

The apothecary retrieved the vial from his satchel and holding it to the light, checked once more for any impurities. Reaching down, he slowly tilted the tiny ratling's lower jaw and administered the elixir. As the first few drops hit the sleeping patient's tongue, an expression of discomfort crossed its face. Edwyn continued to pour until the vial was empty of its contents. Tinker now frothed at the mouth, as his body was consumed by convulsions. His muscles twitched and jerked erratically and then there was stillness. Thucious looked on expectantly as Edwyn checked for any signs of change. With a sigh the apothecary ran his hand through his dark hair. He could note no considerable changes in the affliction.

"You tried" said Thucious placing a hand on the apothecary's shoulder. "That is all one can do."

Looking down the apothecary started to follow the elf towards the door when a small sound caught his attention.

"B-Boss" whispered the ratling. "B-boss is that you?"

Surprised, both men stopped abruptly and turned toward the bed. Watching as a tiny clawed hand raised, they slowly made their way back to the creature's side.

"Boss, is that you?" asked the ratling again with a touch of coherency in his voice.

"Tink, is that you?"

"Of course it's me, Boss. Who would I be?" stated the ratling as he started to rub his head as he tried to ease the pulsating headache. And then he felt them, first the pointy ears, then the elongated snout, and last the whiskers. "W-wh-what's wrong with me" asked Tink with a shuddering in his voice.

"Stay calm, my friend it will be alright" said Thucious as he could see the horror filling his friend's eyes. "Do you remember what happened to you, Tink? Anything at all?"

Tink's mind was still very cloudy. It had seemed

like he had been lost in the mists of some unending labyrinth. Bits and pieces floated along the edges of his thoughts like phantoms. He vaguely remembered that night. Following the two skulking Gnomes, the baker, a cloaked man. No not a man he thought, a rat, a huge rat but that didn't make sense. He also remembered the sound of softly playing music that floated on the air. It called to him, beckoned him. He told them everything that he could remember from his patchy memories. Thucious and Edwyn listened intently to every detail until Tink had become so overcome with the exhaustion of his ordeal he could barely stay awake. Although the elixir had freed his mind, it had taken a toll on his body, fatiguing it.

"We can talk more later, my little friend. Rest now." said Thucious, placing his hand on his head like a father would a child.

Gathering his satchel, Edwyn and Thucious left the room to the sleeping ratling. Dismissing his sons who stood vigilantly watching the door, he then escorted the apothecary down to the kitchen where they could discuss the relevancy of what had transpired and quench his thirst and appetite. Although numerous family members knew what was transpiring, no one walked the halls. Upon a great wooden table, meat and cheese awaited on a platter next to an exotic vintage of wine and two ornate crystal glasses. Taking his place at the head of the table he offered Edwyn a seat to his left. Filling the two glasses, he deeply sniffed the wine, enjoying its unearthly bouquet, before settling down to discuss what had transpired.

Looking through the apothecary's notes and reexamining the events of the evening had drawn only more questions. They had concluded that although the elixir had a positive effect, it did not completely solve the problem. Also it would need to be tested on an infected creature that did not have Tink's heightened metabolism and since they had only heard of one other infected individual, the tailor's wife would be the only logical choice. So while Edwyn administered the elixir to the other ratling, Thucious would speak to Tink again and investigate the other small folk he mentioned.

The clock tower echoed like a faraway beacon, announcing that it had become sometime past the high moon. Thucious led Edwyn through the elaborate door and back to the warehouse above. The docks seemed different tonight as the waning moon passed its apex or maybe Edwyn was just different somehow. He paid very little attention to the shadowed alleyways as he made his way back to the Green Forest. He contemplated every detail from the evening, from when he had arrived at the courier shop until his departure. He had so hastily sworn an oath to an old associate of his mothers, without thinking it through. Would it be his undoing he wondered? And now he was on a mission to treat the infected, which would have been fine if he wouldn't have had to cause his brother to become involved more than he already had been. Making his way down the alleyway behind the Green Forest, Edwyn arrived at the rear of the shop. Unlocking the door, the apothecary, preoccupied with his thoughts, entered, unaware that his small winged brother curiously watched him from his small ledge before entering himself.

Lifting the enchanted reeds to his lips, he blew, releasing his song as he had done so many times before. But this was no ordinary song, the notes that were released upon the Burrows had purpose, had reason. For only a few would hear them, would answer them. Located in the cellar of a long forgotten home, he watched as numerous afflicted small folk mindlessly obeyed his commands. Using the abilities granted to them by the arcane taint, they relentlessly carved and shaped chambers into the dirt below the Burrows. Pulling back his hood, the creature's deep red eyes moved from ratling to ratling, his own whiskers twitching in the torchlight filled darkness. Two had never answered the call, two that would need to be found before someone could interrupt his plans. Ever since the night he had been infected, he had fought the call, thinking he had gone insane by the curse. Running his hand along the scar that stretched from his ear to his chin, he remembered every detail. At that time he didn't know that he was fighting such an infectious creature. But by the first full moon, he had discovered it too late. Greed had pushed him to kill every member of his party as the transformation set in. Greed, hate, loathing, everything the Hauflin had not truly felt before. Not like this anyways. But that had been years before, long before he had learned control. Now his devious plots took time and planning. He only infected a few, and ruled with an iron claw dispatching those who would not bow. But now through years of patience and study, he had devised a way to transform others into controllable subjects instead of head strong competitors. And all this had started from a little cut.

"M-Master G-Gillian" said Nip, whose gnomish stature added to his rodent features. "Master we could not locate the Hauflin thief. There was no sign of him at his house, sir."

"And the other one, what of her?" asked Gillian as he clutched the railing before him.

"The t-tailor, sir. The problem is he keeps her locked away." said Nip as he stared at the ground, trying not to make eye contact.

Gillian's claws dug deeply into the wood. "Problem," said Gillian a tiny chuckle escaped his rodent-like lips, "the only problem I see is you not doing what I have commanded!"

"B-but sir, we couldn't" stated Nip before he was abruptly cut off.

With a movement quicker than a serpent's strike, Gillian had turned and grasped the Gnome's throat slightly applying pressure that was meant to cause more fear than pain. "Do we have a problem?" he asked as the pressure started to make the Nip's beady red eyes to water.

"No, no s-sir, no problem. We will handle it, just as you commanded." said the terrified Gnome.

Releasing his hand from around the fur covered throat, Gillian turned once more and surveyed the entranced ratlings excavating the shrine. With an evil smirk crossing his lips, Gillian stated "Good."

CHAPTER SIX

Generally the Biggs never ventured deep into the Burrows. It could be their size or just the belief that small folk problems were just that, small folk problems. They lived above, the small folk below. Although the Council of Lords ruled the city in its entirety, they allowed the small folk to somewhat govern themselves, as long as the Watch had its presence there. A council was created which was governed by an appointed magistrate to enforce and settle any disputes that arose. And this magistrate was an old dwarf named Stoten Stonetable, whose rock hard fists had solved more than a few squabbles. He had moved here a decade ago, from the Chasm of Steel, for reasons known only to him. But unlike the other four members consisting of Hauflins and Gnomes, he had the patience to listen and evaluate any situation brought before the council.

Days like these were common in the Burrows. Generally few beseeched an audience with the council for most small folk didn't bother about the daily rituals of government. The bailiff would escort the few petitioners in, mostly who squabbled over vendor rights, before the council. But today was different, today Gillian Worldwalker, a prestigious tradesman, stood awaiting his turn to petition the council. Looking up, Stoten sighed as he shook his head as he was not looking forward to another heated debate with the Hauflin. Gillian on numerous occasions had tried to use his influence to take the Stonetable's place as magistrate.

"Gillian Worldwalker, approach the council with your petition" announced the bailiff as he opened the gate to the small box before the five.

Gillian was dressed in finery uncommon among the small folk from his numerous expensive rings to the exotic silk cloak he wore about his shoulders. Walking into the box, he graciously bowed before the council.

"Good day to you wonderful servants of the Burrows, High and Low of course. I beseech this fine council on information concerning the expansions into the other areas of the city," asked Gillian as he tried to flatter the five.

Stoten's features hardened as he stared at the petitioner with contempt. "As we have stated before, as you well know from numerous prior petitions, that we have made no new decisions about the expansion."

"I only look out for the well-being of my kinsmen, good Magistrate," stated Gillian as he cleared his throat. "I hope that you of all people do not wait on the shirt tails of the Lord Magistrate to make your decisions?" asked the Hauflin as a smirk crossed his face.

By now all of the council members had stopped their side conversations to listen to the banter between the magistrate and tradesman. The veins had started to bare on the dwarf's forehead as his agitation grew. And as the dwarf began to speak, Gillian swiftly turned with a grin and left the box, therefore having the last say in their conversation. Leaving the building, he could almost imagine the gavel hitting the wall as numerous dwarfish curses flew after him.

EDWYN HAD to rely on his brother to administer the elixir to Sari, the tailor's wife. Following his notes exactly, Keebo relayed every detail to his brother from the administering to the moment Sari became lucid. It had taken several hours longer for the seamstress to react to the antidote than the courier, but that had been mostly due to his heightened metabolism. Keebo had stayed with Timbles and Fleur until the early hours of the morning, documenting any changes that had occurred throughout the night. Edwyn knew that his younger brother's thoughts were filled with Fleur anyways, but he also knew the fears that crept into his mind as well. Time seemed to solve all problems, he thought to himself, as he sat enjoying a sweet roll delivered by Cara, the young widow next door who owned the bakery.

His younger brother had done well documenting the information. Running his finger across every line, Edwyn compared every detail to the details contained in his own notes. The events that took place at the Tallbreeches seemed to coincide with what had happened with the first ratling. Sari hadn't remembered much after she had become coherent. Two Gnomes, a cloaked man, and notes of a soothing song that seemed to call to her was all she could remember. And although her mind was returning to her, she kept her ratling form, as Tink did. Keebo also had noted that she had been touched by the arcane, which still was perceived as a lightly glowing birthmark. Two Hauflins, both marked by the Fates. Was this coincidence or something else he thought, as he stuffed the last bite of sweet roll in his mouth? Dipping his quill in the inkwell, the apothecary slowly noted what conclusions he had on the latest piece of parchment. It had been almost dawn when his brother had arrived from the Burrows, and Edwyn had decided to let him sleep. Rolling the parchment and sealing it with wax he then set it aside until it could be delivered to the Darkserpent.

Pulling open the curtain separating the front of the shop from the storeroom, Edwyn meticulously started his daily routine sweeping the wooden planks that covered the floor and straightening the shelves. The sunlight shone through the windows, warming the shop and the rooms above. Walking to the front of the shop, Edwyn watched as the particles of dust sparkled in the sunlight when he swept them from the floor. Propping open the shop's front door, the smells of baking pastries and loaves of bread filled the room. When his brother was taken care of he would have to make time for the beautiful woman next door, he thought to himself with a smile. Returning to the counter he began the day's business with a little prayer and a lot of faith.

Within a few tolls of the clock tower, Keebo had bounded down the stairs into the storeroom, looking for something to appease the beast inside his stomach. Pulling up a stool to the hearth, he slowly removed the iron lid covering the stew that his older brother had put on to simmer earlier that morning. Carefully fishing out a piece of succulent ham from the rue, the Hauflin quickly wrapped it in a piece of rye bread left over from the previous day. The ham melted in his mouth as it worked its way down into his gullet, quieting the growls that had erupted.

Tying his apron around him, the young apothecary exited the storeroom to find his brother filling an order for a young handmaiden, whose mistress still carried twin sons of northern stock and was overdue. Watching him, Keebo knew what would be given, Reliq root for the pain mixed with a little Songweed to speed up the boys' arrival; carefully created based on the handmaiden's information. Looking at Edwyn's list, the tiny apothecary began to collect the ingredients from around the store needed to fill orders. On his third pass by the counter he greeted his brother good morning, as he placed a jar of bee pollen near the other ingredients.

"Morning Edwyn, thank you for allowing me

to sleep in a while," stated the Hauflin, "by the way the stew is wonderful."

"Morning back little brother," said Edwyn with a smile, "and Keebs, the stew is for later, not breakfast."

With a huge grin, Keebo stated "I know!"

"By the way, Keebs, I am glad you are awake. I have something important to deliver and I thought you would be the best one to do it."

"A delivery, I thought I might go see how Fleur, I mean how Sari was faring this afternoon." stated Keebo giving his best disappointed look.

"I need you to do this little brother. It is quite important, but maybe you can head to the Tallbreeches afterward, if you would like?" said Edwyn with an understanding yet stern look.

The bells tolled announcing the arrival of noon. The two brothers sat for a moment to enjoy a bowl of stew, and the ends of an old loaf of bread. The shops seem to slow down about this time of day as most of the common folk broke from their daily grinds to enjoy a bite of lunch. And the two brothers were no different on occasion. They talked mostly about the business of the day, and sometimes the weather. But today Edwyn seemed particularly interested in his brother's attraction to a petite young tailor's daughter who lived off Hobbler's Junction. Edwyn had become father and mother to his younger brother as well, when his mother had passed. Teasingly Edwyn told him that it was good that he found a friend that he could have fun with. They were both getting older and would one day have a family of their own. He just needed to be careful, these were strange times, and potentially dangerous as he thought to himself about his agreement with a particular elf.

Taking their bowls, Edwyn took them to the storeroom and returned with the rolled piece of parchment. Setting back down next to the Hauflin, he handed his brother the document and directed him to deliver it to Master Thucious himself, not a courier or the desk boy. Personally hand it to the Darkserpent himself Edwyn reiterated.

"But I wasn't going to go that way today, Edwyn." stated Keebo as he turned the rolled parchment in his child-like hands. "I was going to use a closer entrance."

"I really need you to do this for me today, little brother. I am trying to help Master Thucious figure out the rodent problem before any more outbreaks arise" said Edwyn. "Anyways you won't be far from the Whalebone or your lass." "Promise me, you will."

"Fine Edwyn, I will deliver it for you. I promise," pouted the Hauflin as he tucked the parchment into his belt.

Outside, the flow of traffic had once again resumed as the common folk finished their noon meals. Business had dwindled as the afternoon went on. The two brothers loyally tended to their customers, for which was their life's blood. Then as the sun crawled its way toward the horizon, the shops across the street cast their shadow onto the Green Forest. Edwyn finished tying the caravan leader's last bundle of herbs with twine, thus ending the business day on a good note.

Keebo had left wearing Edwyn's finest shirt, which had been handed down to him. He had wanted to make a good impression on Fleur, and maybe a better one on her father. Walking down the warm cobblestone streets, the Hauflin felt light on his feet as thoughts of seeing the seamstress filled his head. Passing through the great gates, the tiny apothecary gave his customary nod to the human guard that had been positioned at the gate house. A courtesy which was usually ignored either due to their arrogance or the fact that he was barely a couple feet above the ground. But on the rare occasion he did get a nod back or a smile, he might stop and chat as any Hauflin might do.

One could notice the difference of the districts as they passed through the gates. The smells assaulted Keebo's nostrils as the sea breeze rushed along the streets. Making his way down the Downwater, he came to the three story warehouse where the courier business was located. Numerous children wearing the Darkserpent tabards ran in and out of the entrance like ants on a mission as they carried their deliveries throughout the city. Luckily the small apothecary had grown accustomed to weaving through the traffic caused by the Biggs and their carts. Walking calmly into the fray of ants, he made his way to the front counter where a lanky boy, from what Keebo could estimate, was about his age.

"Evening good sir, I have a delivery for your master." said the small apothecary as he stood on his toes trying to see the counter.

Closing his ledger which was customary, the boy looked over the counter and eyed the Hauflin.

"You may leave any parcel for Master Darkserpent in my care and I will deliver it to him" stated Filpin as held his hand out toward the Hauflin.

Pulling the rolled parchment from his belt, he began to hand it to the youth whom guarded the door like a dragon protecting its hoard. And then he thought to himself about what his older brother had said. "Give it only to the Darkserpent, no one else."

Pushing it back into his belt, Keebo said, "I would really appreciate that, but in that lays the problem. See I have promised, my brother that I would only deliver it to the one and only master of this establishment. Of whom I know quite well and for a very long time. Therefore if you would kindly announce my presence to him, I will not hinder you anymore at all."

Hauflins had the unique ability to annoy almost any one, to include other Hauflins. But in that was the game and Filpin knew that. Annoy until you get what you need from a Bigg or until you are thrown out on your breeches. The lanky youth did not seem to give in easily though because a fourth of his couriers just happened to be of the small folk persuasion.

Pushing his copper rimmed spectacles back into place Filpin ended the game with one word "no". Stepping around the counter, he stationed himself between the Hauflin, whom was attempting to bypass him, and the hallway leading to his master's office.

"I said, no" stated Filpin once more, "and I mean it. He is not to be disturbed."

"Fine!" said Keebo as he threw his hands up. "You win, I will just leave then."

Filpin watched as the Hauflin bounded out the door, but for some reason he knew he would see him again. Taking hold of the silk page keeper, the youth opened the ledger and resumed his routine as he kept a watchful eye on the door.

Frustrated, the tiny apothecary left the couriers and turned up the street. This was going to take far too long. He could tell his brother in the morning that he wasn't allowed to deliver like he asked, but he had promised him. And Keebo hated breaking promises, at least to his brother.

Turning around, he looked at the building. He remembered where Master Thucious' office was, so he counted the number of windows along the first story. One window, two windows and then he saw it. The third window had to be it. Looking both ways down the cobblestone street, Keebo casually walked down the alleyway next to the warehouse, examining the numerous crates along the wall. Spying a couple crates near the window, he slowly began to climb until he was directly under the window that had been opened to allow the sounds of the world outside to enter the office. This would have been so much easier if he could have flown up to the window, he thought to himself. Standing on his tippy toes, chest against the wall, he reached for the window ledge.

"Damn, only a few more inches" the Hauflin muttered under his breath. He didn't have the strength to set another crate on top of the one he stood on. His stature wouldn't allow it. "Come on, come on, there has to be something. Think Keebs, think." Shifting the weight of his haversack around, it came to him. Placing his hand to his forehead, he had finally realized that what was needed had been strapped to his back all the time. Removing his haversack, he placed it on the crate below his feet. It was large enough for a human, and was why he used it to cover the bulge from his wings. Tying one strap around his belt, he slowly stood on the haversack. Reaching up, he had discovered the few extra inches he needed to grab the window ledge. Now he thought, if I can just climb up to the window. Placing his boots firmly against the wall of the warehouse, he dug his fingers deeply against the wooden ledge as he attempted to hoist himself up. Keebo's muscles strained as his wings and tail pushed against the straps holding them in place. As a lone bead of sweat rolled down from his forehead, he finally threw a leg over the ledge pulling his self the rest of the way up.

Looking through the window, he spied the lone elf sitting at his desk, skimming the pages of a huge ledger, but as he watched, the pages of the ledger seemed to turn themselves. Steadying his small body along the ledge, he slowly lifted a tiny hand to the glass and knocked. Then he knocked again, but a little louder this time. Turning his head, the elf slowly looked toward the window. Carefully closing the ledger, the elf slid back his chair and moved toward the Hauflin that was balancing on the other side of the pane of glass.

"Good afternoon, Master apothecary" said Thucious as he slowly lifted the window. "I must ask. Was the front door broken?"

"Afternoon Thucious" answered Keebo as the tingling sensation from being around magic caused the tiny hairs on his neck to stand up, "and no your front door wasn't broken, but your guard dog wouldn't let me in. I told him I knew you, and you knew me, but it didn't matter."

"Aw, I see," said Thucious with a small smile. "He is quite efficient at his job." "So my young and determined friend, what has vexed you so much, as to have you scale my walls and enter through my window?"

"Thucious, I made a promise to Edwyn that I would deliver a letter to you and to you only. He made me promise. So I did, or I was trying to, but he wouldn't let me in."

Thucious studied the Hauflin as he gave his explanation. He could see the sincerity in words for which he spoke. Holding out a hand, he carefully helped the Hauflin from the window as the haversack dangled from its belt.

"Still wearing your brother's hand me downs I

see?" he said as he examined the Hauflin's haversack and shirt.

"I like them and they don't cost anything." the Hauflin said with a smile. "Besides they fit pretty good I think."

The Hauflin walked over and took the seat that sat opposite Thucious'. Carefully he climbed into the wooden chair and faced the elf, who had taken his own chair. Standing up, he quickly pulled out the letter that had been securely tucked into his belt. Leaning over he presented the note to the master courier for inspection. Thucious took the letter, breaking the wax seal with his thumb. Opening it, he quickly scanned the letter's contents and then folded it, placing it into his front pocket.

"Your brother has done a fine thing this day, lad." said Thucious as he patted his pocket. "Give him my gratitude, and let him know that I will be in touch."

"I will Thucious, but I have made good on my promise and now I have to be off." declared Keebo as he held his forearm out in common courtesy.

With a smile, the old elf grasped the Hauflin's arm. Keebo then dropped off the chair and placed his haversack back on. Pushing the chair towards the window to make his exit, the elf raised a hand in objection.

"Young apothecary" Thucious stated stopping the Hauflin mid-step. "Use the front door when you leave, and from now on, please."

With his cheeks starting to blush, Keebo said "I probably should use the front door, don't want harassed by the Watch for climbing out a window, now do I."

Turning around and with a smile the Hauflin slowly pushed the chair back to its original position. Waving at the elf who had resumed his perusing of the large ledger, Keebo stood on his toes and grasped the latch which opened the door to the hallway. Turning with a nod, the apothecary exited the office, closing the door with a click.

Thucious now alone, pulled out the letter from his front pocket and studied it carefully. A worried look crossed his brow as he read Edwyn's note. What was this rat's game, he thought to himself. Whatever it was, it couldn't be good.

WALKING DOWN THE HALLWAY, Keebo followed the lines made by the wooden planks. He noticed numerous children running down the hall, while others entered and exited the rooms along the way. Passing by the counter, he noticed that

Filpin had started to close the shop for the evening.

"Thanks guard dog, Master Thucious said it was alright that I see him," stated the smiling Hauflin as he passed the surprised human, who now stared at him. "He said I should always use the front door from now on, though."

Walking passed the astonished boy, Keebo made his way down the steps, turning in the direction of Whalebone Court. The sun had started to settle on the horizon, casting its reflection upon the sea that flowed into the bay. The Biggs seemed to grow fewer and fewer, as he made his way to the entrance leading off the court into the Burrows. Adding to the other small folk as they joined in the ranks, the apothecary followed the others down the sloping cobblestone to where it met up with Boater's Way. This entrance placed him closer to Hobbler's Junction, but it was a farther jaunt from the Green Forest.

Even though he was different from the other small folk, he still felt at home with them. It was nice not to have to dodge someone three times his height. The largest thing down here he would have to dodge might be a cart pulled by a pony or riding dog. As the apothecary mingled in the stream of others his size, he headed down Boater's Way toward Hobbler's Junction. Music filled the tunnels as numerous bards sang their tunes for the workers finishing their day with a pint of ale. Light from numerous lanterns burned, illuminating the way north.

A lone Gnome pushed his wares passed the apothecary as he entered the junction. Tiny lanterns hung from the posts as he made his way past numerous closed businesses to the tailor's shop. Climbing the small set of steps, Keebo spied the tailor working in his ledger as his daughter, Fleur, folded numerous bolts of fabric. Lightly Keebo lifted the brass knocker and let it fall against the small wooden door. Twice it took before it gained Timbles' attention. The old Hauflin closed his ledger, walked across the room and peered through the front window where he spotted the young apothecary standing on the other side of the door straightening his shirt.

Opening the door slightly, Timbles asked "young Master Keebo, we have closed for the day, can your business wait or have you come once more to check on my lady?"

"Master Timbles, I ...." stated Keebo, stumbling over the right words. "I come to ask if I might be able to visit with Fleur this evening, with your permission of course."

Fleur stood silently watching as her father blocked the door, as if holding an invading horde at bay. She wondered how her father was going to react to this gentleman caller, for it was one of the honorable few since she had turned of age. Maybe, she thought, just maybe this apothecary was braver than she thought.

Looking back over his shoulder, Timbles noticed that his daughter had stopped folding the bolts and waited on his decision. Then with a sigh, he turned toward the young boy standing patiently outside the door.

"I think that as long as your intentions are honorable," explained the tailor, as he once more looked back at his daughter, "I think that would be acceptable."

"Thank you sir, and yes indeed sir, very, very honorable, sir" stated Keebo as the tailor let him through the front door.

"And what have you planned for the evening, young apothecary?" asked Timbles as he eyed the boy.

"I – I thought we" stammered Keebo as Fleur added her own thoughts.

"Father," interjected Fleur. "Father I thought we would meet up with Rosie and Bells and go dancing."

"Dancing huh" stated Timbles as he looked over at the young apothecary.

"Yes father, dancing," stated Fleur as she ran up to give him a hug.

Turning, the tailor eyed Keebo and stated "I presume you will not keep my daughter out too late and act nobly this evening?"

A bead of sweat ran down the back of the young Hauflin's neck, and with a gulp, he agreed.

With a wink to Keebo, Fleur turned and ran toward the back rooms to collect her things. Timbles went back to finishing his the closing of the day's accounts, while Keebo slowly meandered around the shop. Bolts of fabric lay stacked around the room as baubles and buttons hung from the racks. The young apothecary would meticulously run his finger along the bolts of fine velvets and silks, imagining what finery would be created from them in the future. On his second tour around the shop, Fleur came bounding from the back, dressed in her traveling clothes, with a small haversack thrown over her shoulder.

Hugging her father goodbye, she grabbed Keebo's hand and headed toward the door.

"Don' wait up, father," Fleur said with a grin as she looked back over her shoulder. With a wave, the two vanished out the door into the evening.

CHAPTER SEVEN

*T*he bells of the clock tower tolled one strike after midnight. Above the watch patrol enjoyed a relatively quiet evening as they turned the corner, ushering the late night revelers toward their homes, but below in the shadows cast by the moonlight that flowed through one of the relatively large air vents, it was different. Tonight, two scraggly Gnomes, under the cover of carefully placed illusions, crept their way into Hobbler's Junction.

"There it is" said Nip as he pointed a gnarled clawed finger towards the tailor shop. "She is in there."

Nip and Tunks moved within the edges of the shadows as added protection in case their illusions failed. Moving quietly along the street, they moved up the tiny steps, to the front door.

"Watch the street, Tunks, as I open the door." stated Nip, who was inches taller than the other.

While Tunks watched down the street and across the junction, Nip slowly pulled out his rusty dagger and slipped it between the door and the jam. Wiggling the blade backwards and forwards, he slowly worked the latch holding the door closed. And then with a low pop, the latch had released and the door slowly opened. Hurriedly, the two Gnomes clambered into the shop, quietly shutting the door behind them.

"Where she at, Nip?" asked Tunks in a low raspy voice.

"Shush, they will hear us. They're probably asleep. Now be quiet." Nip said as he looked around the room.

Moving toward the back of the establishment, they found the Tallbreeches' living quarters. From room to room they searched, looking for the sleeping couple, until they came to a door that was slightly ajar. Silently Nip pushed the door open to get a better look.

"There they be," he said as he brought a clawed finger to his lips. "You get her I will take care of him."

Nodding, Tunks licked his lips and moved over

next to the sleeping ratling. Still cloaked in their illusion, the larger of the two quickly reached down and grabbed the tailor as he slept. The violent act ending his illusion brought him into the bewildered sight of the tailor. Hazily the tailor's eyes opened to the sight of the rodent-like monstrosity that loomed over him. Trying to fight past the shock, the Hauflin tried to rise from the bed, causing the intruder to change his footing. Nip and Timbles rolled to the floor as the brute tried to restrain the aging tailor, knocking over the nightstand.

"Who, what are you?" yelled Timbles as they wrestled. "Run Sari, run!"

"Shut up you runt," growled Nip, as he struck the Hauflin with his clawed fist.

A scream erupted from the other side of the bed, as Tunks reached down, grabbing the surprised female. Struggling against the strong grasp of the Gnome, Sari tried to escape, but she did not have the strength to break free from his grip.

Trying to keep an eye on his beloved, Timbles didn't see the strike coming from Nip. The clawed fist struck again, this time hitting Timbles squarely in the chest, knocking the wind from his lungs. It was hard to catch his breath. Timbles could see stars at the edge of his vision. Reaching up, the

Hauflin fought against his adversary with what adrenaline he could muster. Grasping the clawed hand that held his nightshirt, he bit down hard, bringing the warm taste of blood to his mouth.

"Damn you!" snarled Nip as he let go of the tailor. "You'll pay for that!"

As the tailor tried to turn and crawl away, Nip reached out, entangling his gnarled fingers into the Hauflin's thinning hair. Yanking with all his strength, he nearly snapped the tailor's neck in two. Pulling him to his feet, Nip's ferocity was beginning to bare. More of his own rodent-like features manifested as his anger and control wasted away. Looking at his comrade, who held the horrified Sari in his clutches, Nip reached around the tailor's throat, and digging his claws deeply into the Hauflin's flesh, tore his windpipe allowing the tailor to fall lifeless to the floor.

"No witnesses," snarled Nip as his face contorted into an evil gleam.

"No, no, no" sobbed Sari as they began to bind and gag her.

"If you don't want to end up like him, you'll be stopping the whining little ratling. The master has use for you." stated Nip as he started wrapping a blanket snugly around her. Tying the ends together, Nip looked at Tunks, who had started rifling through their drawers.

"We are not here for that, Tunks. Grab her and come on."

"Didn't hurt anything and he doesn't need it anymore!" snarled Tunks as his whiskers twitched in the air.

The larger ratling's red eyes pierced his cohort. A look of anger crossed his face as he curled his clawed hand, grasping the handle of his rusty dagger. The other ratling, understanding that he may have pressed his luck a little too much, let out a small growl as he conceded to the will of the larger. Reaching down with his own clawed hands, Tunks carefully threw their quarry over his shoulder that was still bundled in the blanket. Following Nip's lead, he made his way to the front of the shop. Casting their illusions, Nip slowly peeked through the door and scanned the area around the junction. The green light from the Watch's patrol lanterns slowly faded as the patrol rounded the corner heading down Boater's Way to the Low Burrows. Counting a few heartbeats, Nip signaled to his counterpart to exit the shop. Making their way, they quickly moved within the shadows up Sparkling Rock in the opposite direction of the patrol. Moving as quickly as they could, they made their way to the home of their master, the Worldwalker.

Carrying her into a room, Tunks slowly

unwrapped the blanket from around the female. Hands bound, Sari stood between the two scraggly Gnomes, who had regained their original forms. In front of her sat a Hauflin with dark, compelling eyes at an exquisite desk covered by numerous scrolls and maps.

"My dear, I am appalled that we had to meet like this, again" stated Gillian, who had risen to his feet and walked over and grasped her hand, "but I am in need of your particular talents of identifying arcane touched individuals."

"Talents! You killed my Timbles, you bastard, my precious Timbles!" cried Sari as tears began to stream down her face once more.

"Yes your talents are needed, but I don't know what you are talking about. I haven't killed any" stated Gillian as he caught a look from Nip who stood shaking his head.

Dropping Sari's hand, Gillian walked to the larger of the two Gnomes. His eyes seem to cut right through Nip's very essence.

"What happened?" snarled Gillian as his fingers started to tremble.

"The tailor didn't cooperate, sir. He had an accident." stated Nip as he tried to not meet his master's stare.

"An accident!" yelled Gillian as his backhand crushed the bones in Nip's jaw.

Pain radiated from the blow delivered by the Hauflin. Dropping to his knees, the Gnome now stood eye to eye with his Hauflin master. Reaching out, Gillian grabbed Nip by the jaw and squeezed it tightly which brought tears to the Gnome's eyes.

"If your actions, this night, have disrupted my plans, I will personally see that you have an accident!" snarled Gillian as he gave one final jerk on the Gnome's broken jaw.

Backing up, he turned and grasped Sari's chin as well. "My dear, I apologize for the misfortune that has happened to your husband, and I would hate for it to happen to you as well. Do you understand?"

The frightened ratling didn't look into his eyes, as thoughts of Timbles were followed by the fear of what could happen to their daughter. All she could do was nod.

WITH FLEUR IN THE LEAD, the two young Hauflins made their way up Sparkling Rock, past numerous inns and taverns. Keebo asked her several times where they were heading, but she only smiled as she led them towards the dock entrance. Up the slanting slope they walked, until two Hauflins popped into view. A dark haired stout leaned against the wall and a small petite female twirled to music only she could hear. Quickening her pace, Fleur ran up and hugged the dark haired stout, whom Keebo recognized as Bells, even though they had never actually been introduced. That would mean that the dainty female would be Rosie. Walking up to the stout, the apothecary presented his hand but to his surprise Bells wrapped his muscular arms around him, picking him off the ground.

"So you're trying to be Fleur's new beau, huh" stated Bells as he gave the apothecary a squeeze and Fleur a wink. "Well I don't know, you're kind of scrawny."

"Bells, leave him alone" said Rosie as she playfully punched him in the side, allowing for the apothecary's feet to once more touch the ground. "We're all small compared to you" she giggled. And she was right, Bells was only slightly shorter than a Gnome, and twice as strong as any Hauflin the apothecary had seen.

"So Fleur, what do you have planned for tonight's jaunt into the city?" asked Bells as he gathered his leather bag from the ground.

"Tonight" looking at the apothecary, "tonight we're off to a fancy soiree amongst the rich and overly indulgent."

"A swar-yae," stated Bells as he looked over at Rosie.

"A party," said Rosie "we are going to a party."

Fleur grabbed Keebo's arm and pulled him along as the others followed. Along the sloping cobblestones they went until they exited into a small park located just off the Twilight Glade. Looking out of the park and across the way, the four Hauflins were dwarfed by the noble households that lined the streets. Old names dotted the cityscape as the newer trade houses came into power. Following the Twilight Glade, they traveled north towards Barrett Street where lively music flowed from a large manor house that had recently had its architecture updated. Large garden lamps lit the grounds which laid hidden behind even larger stone walls. There revelers frolicked in masks, playing the games that nobles played. But instead of heading to the ornate ironwork gate that the guests entered through, Fleur led them to the small manor that sat vacant next to it. Staying in the shadows and dodging the numerous carriages as they crossed the street, the four Hauflins made their way around the stone wall to the service entrance situated down an alley towards the back. Looking both ways, Fleur quietly pressed against the waist high wooden gate, or at least waist high to a human. The wooden planks that made up the gate were in desperate need of repair, but held steady as the opening yielded only the slightest before catching on the chain that bound it closed.

"Drat," whispered Fleur as the gate she pressed against gave no more give. "I didn't count on that."

"Count on what?" asked Keebo as he looked towards the gate.

"I assumed we could sneak in this way since the place was abandoned," stated Fleur as she again pressed on the gate.

"Well I guess we will have to find some other place to go dancing?" stated Keebo as a look of relief crossed his brow. The young apothecary didn't fancy the idea of breaking and entering.

A hand reached from behind and softly touched the apothecary's shoulder, getting his attention. Smiling, Rosie had him step aside while Bells moved closer to the gate and cupped his hands. Placing her foot securely in Bells strong grasp, the stout heaved the lithe female over the gate quickly as to not draw attention.

Leaning closer to the gate, Fleur softly asked, "Rosie you okay? What does it look like?"

The sound of metal scraping metal could barely be heard as the sounds of footsteps echoed towards the alley's entrance.

"Hurry Rosie, the Watch is coming!" said Fleur

as she watched the green light of the Watch's lantern get brighter.

Still there was no reply from the female Hauflin that held their lives in her hands, only the clinking of chain links could be heard from the oppressive gate. Keebo's hands grew sweaty as his tiny heart started to pump adrenaline through his veins. Small iridescent blue lines of arcane energy started to spider web themselves out from his heart, causing a small glow to radiate from beneath his shirt. He would need to calm himself down he thought as he stood motionless between Fleur and Bells. If this was any other night he would soar from this spot to the safety of the roof tops, but he couldn't risk exposing himself.

The green glow from the lanterns inched its way down the stone walls toward the anxiously waiting trio. Pushing their tiny bodies against the gate, the Hauflins did their best to flatten themselves, reducing the chance for the patrol to spot them. Keebo slowed his breathing as he counted slowly backwards, allowing the arcane infused adrenaline to slow disperse. One breath then two, they watched as the light illuminated the alleyway. Then behind them the gate slowly opened as Rosie loosened the lock holding the chain together. Quickly Fleur, Keebo and Bells climbed through the gap created under the loosened chain into the back yard of the manor.

Shutting the door as the patrol grew closer, Bells slowly watched for them to pass the servants' entrance.

"Whew," Bells sighed as he turned toward Rosie. "Cutting it a little close didn't you, my sweet?"

"What, we had plenty of time" stated Rosie as she tucked the last lock of her auburn hair behind her ear. "Weren't scared was ya?"

"Not I," said Bells trying to puff out his chest as his erratic breathing subsided. "Just saying it was too close for comfort."

Smiling the auburn haired Hauflin ran up to Bells and threw her arms around the brawny Hauflin while softly whispering "my hero" in his ear.

With the gate now secured, the tiny band of intruders made their way passed the stables toward the rear entrance of the abandoned manor. A weathered fountain, which sat in the middle of the courtyard, had become the residence of numerous bullfrogs. The young apothecary pictured water gushing from the spout that allowed the frolicking cherub's vase to overflow into the basin below. But in reality, the melancholy cherubs seemed to only stare into a distant horizon. The yard had not been kept for a long time, he thought, as they drew closer to the back door. The stout moved to the front of the line as he checked the door. It as well had been locked, but this time they were not in a predicament that needed to be hastily performed. Kneeling down, Bells allowed his auburn haired beauty to climb upon his shoulders. Then, climbing to his feet, he slowly balanced her on his shoulders so she would be level with the lock.

Rosie eyed the rusty lock that had been built into the door. Her tiny hands meticulously reached into her satchel, producing two picks, no more than wires that had seen better days. Slowly she slid the straight pick into the top of the lock, carefully raising the tumblers. One, two, three tumblers she counted and then she inserted the thicker pick with a curved end into the lock. Placing her boots firmly against Bells chest for balance, Rosie slowly twisted the thicker pick, which allowed the locking mechanism to slip past the tumblers. And with a click, the fruits of her skills became apparent.

With a smile she softly tapped Bells on the head, signaling the stout to slowly kneel down so she could dismount off his shoulders before opening the door. Once on the ground, Rosie placed her picks back into her satchel as Bell started to carefully open the door.

"Do you think we should be doing this, Fleur" asked Keebo with a concerned look on his face. "What if the Watch catches us?"

"We'll be fine, we are just going to do a little exploring before we go to the dance that's all" stated Fleur as the other two eyed the apothecary. "Anyways the Lady of the house passed away and I heard there weren't any heirs."

Keebo sighed as he surrendered to his innate curiosity as well as his feelings to stay with Fleur. He feared getting caught but he feared being branded a coward by the girl he adored even more. Reluctantly he agreed to go in, following Bells and Rosie as they entered the manor, making their way into the kitchen. Cloth covered numerous pieces of furniture throughout the manor. As they went along, his three companions slowly started to acquire numerous pieces of silverware and small trinkets which slowly made their way into their satchels and haversacks. Keebo eyed the building, as he would sometimes feel the tiniest of tingles on the back of his neck. Somewhere in this house there must have been traces of magic. Slowly the group made their way to the second floor where they entered into a long hallway with red carpet that used to be plush and soft, but now only crunched beneath the soles of their tiny leather boots. Along the wall numerous life size portraits looked down upon their uninvited visitors and as the Hauflins passed they would sometimes pause and stare at the manor's previous residents. Then they would resume checking the doors and the rooms, searching them for their hidden treasures.

Making their way down to the end of the hallway, they came to a set of embossed wooden doors. The doors portrayed a couple embraced under the stars sitting in a long forgotten meadow. Slowly Bells reached up and carefully opened the door. The latch was oddly pristine in condition. Entering the bedchamber, the four were amazed to find that the room still stood in immaculate condition. The furniture stood uncovered without the standing of any dust. This room was huge compared to the Hauflins, as they estimated that it was the width of the manor itself. Windows overlooked the street and the courtyard to the rear. Colored lights from the neighboring nobles' festivities cast numerous shadows upon the walls.

Walking around the room, the girls smiled as they adored the decorations in the room as if they had fallen into a princess' dream. Moving from dresser to dresser, they slowly identified any baubles that could easily be taken. Then Fleur discovered a small simple jewelry box that had been carefully tucked away beneath a pile of silk scarves. Opening it carefully, she eyed two beautiful necklaces and a solemn ring. One necklace was gold and silver chains intertwined with each other and the other contained numerous small gems, but the ring was just a plain gold band.

"Eureka" stated Fleur as a smile crossed her lips. Holding them high for the others to see, she carefully placed them in her haversack, as Bells and Rosie watched. Then the tingles seemed to erupt from the hairs on the apothecary's neck. A low rumble came from outside of the bedchamber. Freezing in their tracks, the Hauflins discreetly moved toward the door to get a better look. The hall still was covered in shadows as they stared down toward the stairway. The rumbles, soft at first, seemed to grow in their momentum. And as the rumbling grew, the floor began to tremble. The tingling that Keebo felt had started to greatly intensify, almost numbing his neck. Then a shadow formed at the end of the hallway and moved toward the bedchamber, but not a normal shadow, this shadow had substance, had form. Slowly it floated toward the door, shifting in and out of existence toward the Hauflins. Bells reached to close the door, but in that instance the creature stretched its shadowy claw out, encompassing the stout, causing him to tremble in fear. And then suddenly the shade disappeared, reappearing in the center of the room, separating Fleur from the rest of the party. Rosie ran to Bells, trying to get him to shake off the fear that had infected him, but as soon as the shade had appeared in the center of the room, Bells had become overwhelmed with the thought of running. And he did, gripped by fear the strongest of the band had taken off down the hallway towards the backdoor, instinctively trying to get to safety. Rosie, looking at Keebo, took off after him, hoping to bring him back to his senses, which left only Keebo to make a choice. He wouldn't leave Fleur he thought, but how could he save her against this insidious creature.

"Get away from her" he yelled as the shade grew closer to the woman he loved. The adrenaline pumped liked a roaring river through his veins, causing the arcane spider webs to branch out throughout his body. Watching as the same shadowy claw embraced Fleur, he could see that she had started to tremble as she fought the effects of the shade's fearful touch.

"Mine" stated the creature, but not with words but with its thoughts. Its voice sounded like the wind, which seem to penetrate their minds. "It's mine" it stated again.

The apothecary's could no longer disguise the

power illuminating from his skin. With every heartbeat his wings and tail pressed against their leather bindings, wanting to be free. And as the glow grew, Keebo started to gain the attention of the shade.

Turning toward the energy now being projected from the apothecary, the shade loosened its terrifying grip on the tiny rogue and focused its sight on him. The light seemed to draw it toward him or it was the creature's need for living essence that was flowing like an avalanche, Keebo couldn't be sure. But whatever it was he had drawn its attention to him. Then suddenly, a claw made of solidified shadow, came slashing down toward the Hauflin, cutting his shirt and severing part of the binding that held his uniqueness in check. With no choice, he tore the rest of his shirt and harness off, allowing for his wings to extend. Fleur stood wide eyed as she beheld the Hauflin, whom she thought, was an ordinary apothecary. She stood speechless as the creature's anger now was being released on someone else, something else. She rubbed her eyes, she couldn't believe. Was this the fear effects she thought? No, no this was real. Her mind swam; it was so much to take in.

Keebo dodged another swing of the solidified claws that radiated cold as they passed. He had to circle around and get to Fleur, who now stood with her jaw dropped.

"Fleur, come on. Snap out of it, I could use a little help!" yelled Keebo as he rolled closer to her, just missing being gored.

Fleur finally began to gain her senses and slowly started to react to Keebo's situation. Closing her eyes, she slowly started to hum, and as she did her own little birthmark started to glow. As she hummed she opened her eyes, reaching out with the power in her own soul, causing numerous tiny items to rise from their resting places. The faster she hummed the quicker the small mirrors, combs and other things began to swirl around the room, causing a perpetual windstorm of objects flying through the air. Many of the items missed the creature, but because they were enchanted, the ones that did hit seemed to bother it. Then a mirror crashed into the wall, sending enchanted shards toward the creature, striking it in numerous places, which stuck in the creature's semi-solid form. For a second the creature wasn't horrifying but terrifyingly beautiful as the shards shimmered in the shadow stuff that sustained its body. And then it was gone, if only to allow the shards to drop to the floor from its body.

It was at that moment the apothecary bolstered his courage and at that instance he ran to Fleur and pushed her toward the windows. Picking her up in his arms, he flapped his wings, hurling them towards the glass doors at the rear of the room. And as they shattered the glass, he felt a sharp slice to his back that sent a cold chill down his spine, but he didn't look back. He only kept looking forward as he barreled through the glass, holding the rogue tightly. From the shattered glass door, the shadowy creature looked on in agony before it retreated in from the balcony. Below, two frightened Hauflins watched as an iridescent winged creature exploded from the room and carrying off their friend.

CHAPTER EIGHT

*P*ain pulsed through his body with every flap of his wings, causing the young apothecary to adjust his grip for fear of dropping the rogue. Scanning the area, Keebo made his way some distance before landing on the shingled roof of a small two story warehouse. His muscles ached and the stiffness in his wings had caused them to dip numerous times in flight, and every time, Fleur would gaze upon him with a hint of fear. Hovering above the roof, he slowly lowered the girl down upon the wooden shingles before himself tried to land. And land he did. Descending, his strength gave way, and he landed haphazardly, panting as his energy seemed to be draining away.

"You're the Imp!" stuttered Fleur as she sat down upon the roof, keeping an eye on the Hauflin before her. "It was you all along, the one who saved me in the docks?"

"Fleur" stated Keebo as he slowly tried to rise to his knees. "We need to keep moving."

Fleur watched as a softly glowing stream of blood trickled down the Imp's back down upon the roof. From her position she could see a sharp gouge running down his back, but to her amazement the cut had started to slowly knit itself back together as if the wound had a mind of its own. She still had trouble wrapping her thoughts around the reality that had begun to unravel in front of her. She was looking at the infamous Imp, but also she saw the shy apothecary whom she thought would be brought out of his non-adventurous life during this evening. And as she stood contemplating the jest of all that had happened, she failed to notice that the apothecary had crawled up the roof and set his back against an old dormer.

"Fleur, are you alright?" asked Keebo as he watched her just standing there; her mind in some other place. "Fleur," he yelled trying to bring her back.

Blinking, she arrived back to reality and looked at him. Slowly making her way up the roof, she sat down next to the Imp, whose body slumped against the dormer without saying a word.

Staring out over the roof top Fleur said again, "you're the Imp."

"I guess so. So where does this leave us, Fleur?" asked Keebo as a frown began to cross his face.

Fleur turned and looked at the Hauflin who sat beside her. "I guess I always knew, maybe not for sure. But I wondered. It was your eyes. I didn't know where I had seen them before, but I do now."

"And are we okay, Fleur," asked the apothecary. "I know I am a monster, I just hoped I would get to tell you differently. I don't want you to be afraid of me."

Looking at him, she could see her reflection in his silvery blue eyes. She didn't fear him though, she felt unusually calm for once. He had saved her on more than one occasion and now he was in pain. She watched as the iridescent blue spider webs melted away, receding back to his heart.

"Let me look at your back, Keebs" stated Fleur as she slowly leaned toward him.

"Don't worry about me, Fleur," said Keebo. "It's only a scratch."

"Nonsense," she exclaimed as she remembered how bad the gash had been.

Leaning him forward, she began to inspect the cut, but to her amazement the opening had almost completely closed, leaving only the faintest mark. She slowly drew her finger along the scar and then along the fleshy wing closest to her. They reminded her of a bat's wings for they were the only ones she could compare them to. And as she ran her finger over the tiny hairs that covered it, her soft touch sent a shudder over him.

"It looks like it is almost healed," stated Fleur as she had him lean back. "But how?"

"It's a knack I have" said Keebo as he sat back against the dormer catching his breath. "I have always healed quickly, but my strength will take a while longer to return fully."

The two sat on the roof and discussed all that had transpired as of late, until the stars started to fade into morning. Realizing that they would need to be on their way before the first rays hit the city, Keebo stood up and held out his hand to the rogue. He had already decided that if she refused him, it was meant to be. But instead of turning away from him, Fleur graciously took his hand and climbed to her feet.

"But what if you are seen?" she asked.

Smiling, Keebo looked into her eyes and stated, "I have a plan for that."

Hand in hand they worked their way from the dormer to the edge of the roof. Wrapping his arms around her, he took a step off and the pair plummeted towards the cobblestone pavement. Then at the appropriate time, he opened his wings and flapped them gaining altitude. Fleur had never believed she would be flying over the rooftops of the city, but tonight she was. Keebo's wings spread, holding them aloft on the air currents that whistled through the streets and alleyways until he spotted a clothesline supported by two small iron clad balconies. Slowing circling the alleyway, the two Hauflins cautiously descended between the stone walls, alighting on one of the balconies. Pulling on the line, Keebo carefully pulled the clothing that hung there towards his balcony. The pulleys creaked with every pull on the line, inching the clothing closer. As the clothing came toward the pair, he would quietly unhook each piece until he acquired a shirt that would fit him correctly. He hoped that the Bigg wouldn't need it and he might even return it someday, but that would definitely be for another night. The shirt felt like a burlap sack that had been washed numerous times, but it would have to do he thought. Untying the end of the clothesline, Keebo quickly used the slightly jagged edge of the metal balcony to cut the line. It took a few minutes to do so, but he diligently worked the line back and forth until the edge gnawed its way through. Then with Fleur's help, he wrapped the piece around him like a makeshift harness, securing his wings and tail to his back. The shirt was huge compared to the Hauflin and might have swallowed even his big brother. Pulling it over his shoulders, the small apothecary was engulfed by the hand sewn shirt. Next he tied the remaining clothesline to the railing of the balcony, so that they might have a way to safely descend to the cobblestone streets below. Patiently he waited as the rogue slowly lowered herself down the clothesline, while he maintained a watchful eye for the guard or any other predawn travelers, and then he followed.

Making their way out of the alley, they quickly headed toward the Bilpinboggle cargo elevator which was used during the day to transport large crates of goods from the docks to the Burrows; cargo that would generally not fit through the narrow streets and tunnels. At the bottom, traders and merchants could slowly off load their wares into their small carts and wagons. Luckily for the two Hauflins, during their mad flight from the manor, they had crossed the boundary dividing the Nobles' manors and the docks, bringing them closer to the shaft.

Silently making their way to the elevator, the two Hauflins slowly peered around the corner, keeping a watchful eye on the guard who sat with his back against the wall napping. Trying not to kick up dust as they ventured closer to the platform, the two skirted the small guard post and its sleeping protector. Slipping under the small wooden swing gate that protected the elevator, Keebo and Fleur situated themselves for the descent into the Burrows below.

"Are you ready, Fleur?" whispered Keebo as he reached up with both hands and grasped the lever.

With a nod, Fleur braced herself against the railing closest to the apothecary. Keebo had never operated this contraption before, so his palms grew slightly clammy as a single bead of sweat trickled down his neck. Taking a deep breath, the apothecary braced himself for the ride. With the lever in his hands, he slowly jerked down, trying to release the mechanism. To his surprise though, it didn't move. Placing his tiny boot against the base of the elevator, he mustered his strength and pulled again, but this time the pulleys started to squeak as they began to release the ropes, allowing the platform to descend. Then the platform picked up speed, causing the pulleys to no longer squeak, but to squeal in a loud shrill as the elevator felt as if it was plummeting toward its final destination.

Pushing up on the lever, Keebo tried to accommodate the descent by slowing the platform down, but without his arcane intensified adrenaline his normal strength was lacking.

Looking back over his shoulder he yelled to Fleur to grab the lever and help him push it back up. The rogue haphazardly worked her way to the apothecary's side and with all her might helped to gradually raise the lever, allowing the elevator to slow as it arrived at its final resting place. Dust flew up as the platform landed in the Burrows. Both Hauflins, breathing heavily, stared at each other, before they embraced, savoring their victory over surviving their first use of the cargo elevator. Climbing under the adjoining swing gate, they hurriedly departed from the area as the smell of burnt grease and shrilling pulleys announced their arrival to the Burrows and the patrolling watchmen.

Expediently they moved down the street, making their way to Hobbler's Junction and Fleur's father's shop. The junction was still empty but soon it would be thriving with different patrons and street vendors, forming the largest bazaar in the Burrows. Crossing the street, the two made their way to the front door of the shop, but then something caught the rogue's eye.

"Keebs, the door is open" stated Fleur as she pointed to the door that stood slightly ajar.

"Maybe your father just forgot to lock it, or maybe he left it open for you," said Keebo as he watched her examine the opening.

"Not my father, he knows I always carry my key. And look," she said as she pointed toward the lock, "someone has forced the door open. Look at the scratches on the door jam."

Peering down where her fingers moved across the scratches, Keebo watched as she slowly grasped the door handle and opened the door. The front of the shop looked normal with nothing out of place. Quietly they moved toward the back where her family's living quarters were located. With the apothecary in tow, the rogue carefully moved from room to room until she noticed that her parents' bedchamber door was slightly open. Pushing the door open only a crack, she saw that the room was in shambles. Throwing the door open the rest of the way, she could barely make out the silhouette of something, no someone lying partially obscured by the nightstand that had been overturned. Moving carefully toward the body, butterflies erupted in her stomach, causing her to become nervous. It was hard to see in the darkened room, until the apothecary found an oil lamp lying on the floor, leaking its precious fluid on the baseboards. Scrounging about the floor, Keebo finally found the small tinder box that the Tallbreeches had used to light it. And as he lit the lantern, Fleur's saddened cries could be heard in the darkness. As the lantern's light dispelled the room's darkness,

Keebo observed the rogue, cradling in her lap, the head of her father whom laid motionless on the floor, as a small puddle of blood served as a marker of where his head had come to rest.

"Oh father," whispered Fleur, as tears streamed down her tiny face.

Shadows danced around the room that lay in shambles. Keebo tried to console Fleur, who seemed consumed by the agony of her father's death, but her tears poured like a mountain stream in the spring time. And although she sat on the floor sobbing, thoughts raced through his mind until they settled on one particular revelation.

"Fleur, where is your mother?" he asked as he moved to the opposite side of the bed.

"What" stated Fleur as she still sat in shock of their discovery?

"Where is your mother, Fleur?" Keebo asked again, but this time in a manner that would draw her back out into reality. "She isn't here."

"She isn't here?" stated Fleur as she took a glance around the room.

Laying her father's head gently upon the floor, she slowly rose to her feet, wiping away her tears on the flowing sleeve of her tunic. Keebo carefully draped a handmade blanket over Timbles' battered body before beginning the search of the home. Taking Fleur's hand, he slowly led her out the room and down the hallway. Desperately they searched each room looking for Fleur's mother, but to no avail. She was gone without a trace.

Turning to Fleur, Keebo sighed. "Fleur we need to get some help."

"What can the Watch do? Mother is missing, father is," taking a deep breath, "is gone."

"No Watch, no guards, I have someone else in mind, Fleur. Someone who can help, but we need to leave now."

"I can't leave him, Keebs, not alone. Not like this."

"This is our only hope," said Keebo as he held her hands, trying not to focus on the tears that stained her cheeks. "We won't leave him for long."

Staring back at the room where her father's body laid, she knew down deep the apothecary was right. They needed help, she needed help. With Keebo in the lead, she followed him down the hallway and past the bolts of materials that lay stacked in her father's shop. Securing the front door as best as they could and making sure they were not being followed, they quickly made their way to the city above, exiting the Burrows at the Whalebone. The sun peaked over the eastern horizon, its rays slowly beckoned the new day. It had not yet chased away the mists that crept along the streets of the docks, but that hadn't stopped numerous travelers trudging their way to work. Dodging wagons full of goods and numerous Biggs on foot, the two desperately made their way to the courier shop. Climbing the steps, Keebo slowly reached up and grasped the handle, opening the front door. Soft chimes filled the air as the sound of footsteps echoed down the hallway. As usual Filpin worked his way to the front desk where he spied the young apothecary.

"You again," he began as his eyes fell on the weary Hauflins. "What in the Hells happened to you two." Tired and dirty, the two exhausted travelers looked up at the boy leaning over the desk.

"We need to speak to Master Thucious, Filpin." stated Keebo. "We need his help."

The lanky youth had learned a long time ago how to tell when a person fell on dire times. He explained that the boss would be here momentarily, but they would need to wait. Keebo turned to Fleur and grasped her hand, while a lone tear fell, following the worry lines that seemed to mark her cheeks.

"It will be okay Fleur, we're safe here. Thucious will know what to do."

CHAPTER NINE

*F*ilpin watched as the small apothecary sat trying to console the smaller female. Soon Thucious would arrive and relieve him of this melancholy ordeal. While he kept an eye on the Hauflins, he maintained his daily duties preparing for the day's new business. Numerous children passed by the Hauflins as they bounded from the building carrying their missives and parcels throughout the city. Hearing the door at the end of the hall softly open and close, Filpin turned in time to observe Thucious entering his office. Allowing a few moments for his boss to acclimate himself into the role of Master Courier, he slowly slipped away from the front desk and proceeded to deliver the news of the visitors to Thucious.

"Good morn Filpin," stated the silver haired elf as he stuffed the last morsel of biscuit into his mouth. "What's wrong?"

"Morning Boss," stated the lad. "You have some visitors, who look like they have had a rough night. They have been here since I opened the door."

"Who are they, boy?"

"The small apothecary from the Green Forest, and some small female I haven't seen before, sir. He looks tired and she has been crying, a lot."

"I see and did they happen to mention what misfortune had befallen them?" asked Thucious as he straightened the stack of new broadsheets.

"No sir, he asked only that they be allowed to speak with you most hastily."

A concerned looked crossed his old elven brow, what could have happened to cause two young Hauflins to cross his threshold so unhappily. "Show them in, Filpin and make sure we are not bothered for a while, lad."

With a nod, the lanky youth left his master's office and proceeded to return, escorting the two Hauflins. Down the hall, they traveled until they arrived at the old wooden door leading into the office. Opening the door, Keebo's mood seemed to brighten as the Darkserpent stood awaiting their arrival.

"Young Master of the Green Forest, what vexes

thee so early in the morn?" asked Thucious as he placed a hand on the young apothecary's head. "It looks as though you both have had a rough night."

Climbing up on the chairs that sat reserved for his business associates, the two Hauflins looked at the master courier with silent pleas.

"What has happened?"

"Master Thucious, she's gone, and Timbles is" stated Keebo, "is dead!"

A concerned, more than a surprised look crossed the old elf's face. Thucious listened as the young apothecary recounted his tale of the prior evening, paying specific attention to the elaborate details encompassing the tailor shop. Step by step he had the apothecary walk him through the events. Then he asked numerous questions that helped him fill in the empty hours of the night. When the young apothecary missed a detail, his petite friend piped up between dried tears, adding to the story. As the details swirled in his mind, he had barely noticed when Keebo asked him a question.

"Thucious, what do we do next?" asked the young apothecary, "Master Thucious."

"Oh yes lad. What to do next?" stated Thucious as he was drawn out of his thoughts to the two Hauflins that sat wide eyed looking for direction. Rising from the seat he had taken on the edge of the desk, Thucious slowly rubbed his chin with an insightful look. "First you and your friend should return to the Green Forest and get some rest, also explain what has transpired to your brother, Edwyn. Do not go back to the tailor shop! Stay there until you here from me."

"But my father, I need," stated Fleur who was abruptly cut short.

"You will do as you are told little one!" stated the master courier sternly. "Second lass, I will take care of your father and check into your mother's disappearance."

"But," Fleur started to rebuke as Thucious shot her a soul piercing gaze which ended her argument before it started.

A knock on the door broke the silence shared between the three. As the door opened, Filpin stood waiting to escort the Hauflins down the hall and out onto the cobblestone street. With a gracious nod, the young apothecary climbed down from the chair and stretched his hand to Fleur who descended from her own wooden chair.

"Remember you two, do nothing in haste until you hear from me," stated Thucious as he looked directly at the female Hauflin.

As Filpin led the two down the hallway, the old elf sat down behind his desk and scribed a message to an old friend of his that made his home deep within the confines of the Temple of Feydosha.

Philos,

A good fellow and one of your kin has lost his life defending his home in the Burrows and is in need of the proper rites as he passes from this life to the next. I ask that you accept my call to quietly acquire his remains and ward his home from further intrusion until some retribution is awarded. He slumbers at the Tallbreeches off Hobbler's Junction. As always the debt accrued will be paid, especially if he has anything important to share.

With haste and diligence,

Thucious

Folding the letter, Thucious then placed the Darkserpent seal within the wax he dribbled upon it, forming a seal. As he sat waiting for Filpin to return and the seal to harden, his thoughts examined the details that the young apothecary had bestowed upon him. In general, kidnapping for ransom, might ordinarily have crossed his mind, but he knew that the current condition of tailor's widow made this situation far from an ordinary intrusion. His thoughts seemed momentarily paused as the lanky youth returned from his escort.

"I have need of Jes, Filpin. Is she around this morn?" asked Thucious.

"Yes sir, she arrived shortly after you met with the Hauflins."

"Send her in to me, lad. I have a special task for her. And Filpin."

"Yes boss?" the boy said as he began to turn and leave the office.

"Send word to all our ears in the Burrows that a rat is skulking around and I want to know why?"

Filpin nodded and sprinted down the hallway, looking for the spirited small folk courier. And after a short time, the small Gnome known by Jes, flitted in to the master courier's office. Her red hair bouncing passed the desk, as she worked her way up into the chair opposite the wizened elf.

"Did you need me, boss?" asked the cheerful Gnome.

"Jes, I need this delivered to Philos as quickly as possible."

"AH BOSS, that ol'fuddy duddy. He is always in a foul mood," stated Jes as her sunny disposition began to darken.

"Yes, and with haste, my young apprentice." stated Thucious as he handed her the letter.

Jes took the letter and tucked it firmly into her belt before jumping from the chair to the floor.

"And Jes," stated the old elf as he gave her a small smile, "be careful."

Looking back at the master courier, Jes gave him a wink and a sly little grin. "As always, boss."

Then she bounded out of the building, heading toward the Whalebone.

GILLIAN STOOD OVER HIS DESK, examining the lamb skin map that draped over it. Sketched upon the map were outlines of numerous buildings and tunnels that made up the Burrows, but it also contained numerous markers not listed on any other map. Following the text detailing a forgotten chamber, a grin crossed Gillian's lips. It had taken many years of planning, but he could see his prize in sight. Gillian was cold and calculating, not like his Gnome henchmen. They were followers and dimwitted, but they were also subservient and the muscle he needed. In his younger days he had cursed them with the very disease that now drove him in search of immeasurable power and greed, but he had learned from his mistake. Through years of studying abroad, he had discovered how to taint his victims without truly cursing them. The taint transformed them and allowed Gillian to control them without creating another power hungry creature to share his conquests with.

In the past years he had relied on the greed of certain individuals to further his intentions. Some only needed the promise of coin and power, while others were the product of fear and torture. Only two things now hindered his plan. The first was the uncooperative seamstress, whose unique ability to identify the touched allowed him to add power to his converts, and the second was the Stonetable's lack of ambition to further the expansion of the Burrows under the other areas of the city.

But soon none of these things would matter. Soon all would hear the sweet alluring voice of the darkness. She would call to them, beckon to them just like she had done to him after the turn. He would indoctrinate any who would willingly be converted, all the others would be tainted, mindless slaves to the darkness, to She Who Scurries. And in time, when a proper vessel could be found, she would once again walk the realm.

CHAPTER TEN

Surrounded by candles, deep within the lower sanctums of the Temple of Feydosha, a small body lay wrapped in cloth. Here in secret revelation a priest, dressed in a darken cloak, meticulously finished inscribing the divine runes upon the flesh of the deceased Hauflin male that lay upon the raised dais. Admiring his work, Philos, wiped the sweat from his graying brow and sat the ink well back on the small workstation. The elder priest of Mardasha had resided in the lower levels of the temple for many years, hiding his true patronage within the folds of Feydosha's clergy. And although his grumpy disposition seemed to keep most away, his particular set of divine skills proved increasingly useful to some.

Laying a crippled hand upon the deceased

forehead, Philos began to chant in low tones, praying for divine guidance in his endeavor.

"Mistress, grant me your guidance. Fill this body and find the soul, so we may be counseled into his demise."

Smoke slowly drifted from the candles and burning incense, filling the mouth and nostrils of the cloth wrapped corpse. And as the lungs of the decease seemed to inhale the pungent vapors, the inked runes began to glow. Philos understood that he had to work quickly, for when the smoke had been completely exhaled he would be out of time.

Grasping the chin of the corpse, Philos carefully began his questions.

"Are you Timbles Tallbreeches?"

As smoke escaped the dead lips, "yes" could be heard drifting from its mouth.

"Did your lady murder you?" stated Philos, who tried to keep the answer to the questions as simple as possible.

More smoke poured from Timbles' lips. "No" drifted upon the smoke.

"Who killed you, tailor?" demanded the priest as the entirety of the smoke worked itself free from its fleshy container.

The smoke started to rush faster from the body as the corpse's chest seemed to heave from exertion, and as the last few wisps escaped into the ether, Philos could hear the words, "monsters."

The old priest carefully removed his hand from the corpse's chin and slowly sat back contemplating what small bit of information he had gained from the deceased. Closing his eyes he quietly thanked the Lady of Mysteries, and prayed that she would grant sweet vengeance upon whatever "monsters" had taken the man's life. Then he carefully wrapped the corpse's head in strips of cloth, so it could be properly buried by the family. He had painstakingly prepared the body for its last rites, so he could have the time to contact the departed, and with his mistress' blessing had accomplished that task. Philos, turned and dipped his hands into the cool basin of water that sat on the pedestal by the door so he could wash the death from his hands. Drying them off, he next reached for the latch, opening the door which would allow the acolytes to remove the body.

Two stout Hauflins awaited outside the chamber, the smaller of the two absentmindedly pacing from one side of the tunnel to the other. They would carry the body down below to the catacombs where it would be held until the family arrived for its proper burial. Philos smiled at the nervousness of the smaller one, like so many others the business of placing the deceased in the catacombs had unnerved him.

"Lads, be careful and care not to defile this body on its journey below," smiled the old priest as he looked at the smaller boy. "Don't want any spirits to get you."

The smaller acolyte hands trembled as he reached down to lift the cloth wrapped body and grabbed the handles of the stretcher. With a heave they lifted the tiny remnants of the tailor and carried him to his temporary resting place.

SCRAG STOOD motionless as the two dire rats sniffed their way down the hand carved corridor, their whiskers sweeping back and forth in the dark. The deep Gnome's natural ability to blend into his surroundings had saved him numerous times of late. Waiting anxiously as the creatures past, a lonely bead of sweat slowly made its way down his neck to the collar of his rust colored tunic. Generally Scrag wasn't bothered by the scurrying of rats down the tunnel, but these dire rats were as big as riding dogs and extremely more dangerous. After escaping the slavers of the Down Deep, he had stumbled his way into the Burrows, making his home here in the depths of the lowest levels.

Not many of the residents of the Burrows usually bothered him here, as he mucked out a life of scavenging and solitude, but now rats, two and four legged, seemed to use this small tunnel almost constantly, making it hard to stay elusive.

Holding his breath until the rats passed, he watched as they turned down the path leading to the newly excavated sub-basement. When they were out of sight, he slowly exhaled and started to make his way toward the upper levels with his bag of possessions in hand. He didn't like doing business in the levels above, but now he was going to live there. Life had become entirely too dangerous in the tunnels below. Also the idea of being neighbors to a deranged cult of rat monsters didn't set with him either, especially after his cohort, Pebs, was found torn apart one night. Pulling his cloak close about his shoulders, Scrag hurriedly made his way to the next level of burrows, only momentarily stopping as a pack of sewer rats hauled their contraband from drain to drain.

Winding his way through the catacombs of stairs and tunnels, Scrag finally made his way on to Boater's Way. Not many had been as deep as him, and most who did turned out to be lost in the spider web of tunnels. Following the street, he found himself standing in front of *The Pick and*

Hammer, a small tavern owned by an aging dwarf known as Reyrok. The smell of stale mead wafted through the double doors as voices bellowed out from within the Dwarven mead hall. To the common folk, The Pick and Hammer had a reputation of being dirty and rowdy, but to those few who knew her secrets, the hall was a place of back room dealings and a smuggler's get-away. Scrag quickly stepped aside as the doors burst open. Tucked under each arm, Kaern the bouncer, carried two bruised and battered Hauflin drunkards out of the hall. Tossing them to the street, the two dusted themselves off and with a sly grin to one another cheerfully padded their pockets before heading on their way.

With a small nod to Kaern, Scrag stepped passed the dwarf and entered the hall.

"I was wonder'in if you'd make an appearance today, Scrag?" Reyrok stated as he slowly wiped the bar. "Thought you might have ended up like ol'Pebs."

A picture of his friend being torn asunder came to mind as he replied to the old dwarf, "no, but I did have a small run in with some rats on the way here. Tunnels are getting full of them."

"Do we have a deal then?"

"Aye, we do. As long as you work for me, I will

put you up in the back." answered the old dwarf as he reached for a half emptied mug.

Reyrok and Scrag had a beneficial business relationship and the dwarf knew a good deal when he saw it. Scrag was useful for salvaging items from the tunnels, and he wasn't intimidated traveling into the darkness of the Underrealm. Reyrok also knew that the deep Gnome liked to be left alone, and wouldn't draw attention to himself, which made him a valuable resource. Scrag on the other hand, didn't completely trust the aging dwarf, and understood that his livelihood was weighed solely on his usefulness.

Scrag nodded to the dwarf and preceded to cross the dirt covered floor of the common room. The noise bothered Scrag, but he would just have to get used to it, for a while anyways. He already missed the solitude of the tunnels, he thought to himself as he dropped his bag on the stone floor of his new room that sat off the main storeroom. But it was better than living next to the rat creatures, or so he hoped.

CHAPTER ELEVEN

Gillian stood upon the outcropping of jagged stone as the streams of shadowy mist swirled about, encompassing him. In the distance, his Mistress beckoned to him. He longed to join her, her call, like honey, was nectar to his soul. But the mist held him, kept him captive. Then off the ledge of the outcropping, an altar formed from nothingness. Upon it laid a vessel, a female fit for sacrifice as the mist gathered and consumed her. And all the while Gillian could hear his Mistress' voice upon the wind.

"I understand, my Lady" whispered the wererat as he bowed his head, "and obey!"

The voice again could be heard upon the wind, but this time the voice traveled within the fury of a storm. Swirling the mist, concealing the vessel once more. Now in the stars above a great lunar eclipse appeared. Gillian stared at the great illuminated sphere of shadow and light, as he began to be drawn into its vast emptiness. Deeper and deeper he went until he could no longer feel the maelstrom of howling storm. And then just as it had begun he awoke in the solitude of his bedchamber.

Gillian rose from his bed with renewed vigor. He hadn't truly understood what he was to accomplish by unearthing the altar, but he did now. His goal was now clear. And in three days under the lunar eclipse his plan would come to fruition. His hands slightly trembled as he buttoned his vest. It was from sheer anticipation, nothing else. Traveling from his bedchamber down the hallway, he stopped at the room of his house guest. Light poured into the darkened guestroom as Gillian opened the door. Leaning against the far wall, the fatigued body of the seamstress laid in an uncomfortable position. Her plate of food sat overturned on the floor. She had refused to eat again out of protest of her captivity, but that had worked to the wererat's unknown agenda. Walking over to the tiny ratling, Gillian stopped only to announce his presence.

"Good morn my dear, I see you have refused to eat again?"

"I am not hungry," Sari replied as she tried to muster the strength to rise into a more comfortable sitting position. After her repeated refusals to use her abilities to further his goals, Gillian had grown tired and had her shackled in irons.

Reaching down, Gillian softly caressed her cheek as an evil grin crossed his lips. Looking deep into the eyes of the seamstress, he knelt even closer as he spoke. "It's okay now my dear, I don't need your gifts anymore. We have something more special in store for you now. Something much more special!" And with that, he turned and left her there in the dark, shackled and alone.

Making his way to his study, he passed numerous treasures he had acquired over the years. Running his fingers along their displays he relived every adventure it had taken to acquire them. In his study, he slowly approached the stairwell that had been painstakingly hid beneath the trapdoor located behind his desk. Triggering the latch located beneath the lip of his desk, Gillian waited as the sounds of wheels and pins released the door to reveal a small winding staircase. Then he traveled down the small set of winding steps until they opened up into the newly finished tunnel connecting his manor to the tunnels outside of the unearthed alter room. Rats scurried back and forth throughout the hallway, but they never seemed to enter Gillian's study. Gillian made sure of that as he pressed his will upon them. In his mind they held the same status as his Gnome henchmen, useful but still subservient. The sickening smell of his ratling slaves wafted through the tunnel causing the Hauflin's nostrils to flare. Taking a deep breath, Gillian's Hauflin form began to melt away, leaving only his wererat form.

Stepping out into the catacomb of tunnels, he approached the alter room. Tunks sat asleep with his back against the wall, while the mindless slaves laid around the floor in their tattered clothing.

"M-Master," stated the wererat Gnome as one eye slowly opened. "They have finished the excavation, as you commanded."

"Good" stated Gillian as he surveyed the room. "Has there been any more surprises?"

"No sir, just the one deep, we haven't seen any others." stated Tunks with a toothy smile as he thought about the dire rats tearing the deep Gnome apart. "Nip left a short while ago to patrol the tunnels, but he hasn't returned yet."

"Good then. We don't need any other complications in the nights to come," stated Gillian as he rubbed his clawed hands together. His eyes fell on the altar as he imagined the body of the vessel sprawled upon the dais. And as he fought the urge to drag her weakened body down into the tunnels, he could feel the slight tremble again in his hands.

CHAPTER TWELVE

Keebo looked at Fleur as she laced up her leathers. The young apothecary had argued until he was out of breath against her going down into tunnels, but she wouldn't have that. She was too stubborn to hear of it. Maybe he thought, just maybe the Darkserpent would be able to talk some sense into her. They were to meet at his shop, and then as a group they would descend beneath the Burrows together.

"Fleur," Keebo said as he handed her cloak to her, "I, I just." Then his voice just seemed to trail off.

"I know Keebs, I know," stated Fleur as the young rogue's eyes met his. So much to say and no time to say it.

Grabbing his mask from behind the dresser in the alcove that kept it safe, Keebo slid it down over his face. Only his silver blue eyes remained to remind Fleur of his kind and caring soul. Opening the bedchamber door, the two leather clad Hauflins made their way to the garden balcony that held the herbs that Keebo's mother once grew. The young apothecary drew in a deep breath knowing that this could be the final time that he might ever step foot here at the place he called home. Pulling Fleur close, he wrapped his strong arms around her, and looking to the sky, the Imp took flight.

Keebo leveled off his flight and smiled as he looked down at the young rogue who had begun to open her eyes. Fleur's eyes met his and a small smile appeared on her face. For being fearless, the Imp knew that becoming airborne, although exhilarating, still scared her. Holding her tighter, Keebo carried them over the wall into the Docks and to where the Darkserpent waited.

The moon had started to move into position as the lunar eclipse grew closer. Down the two Hauflins descended, landing in the alleyway alongside of the courier shop. The only light in the building illuminated Master Thucious' office window. Walking down the alley past a stack of shipping crates, the two Hauflins were surprised to find Filpin, standing at the door awaiting their arrival. With a nod, he stepped aside and pointed down the hallway to the office.

"The boss is waiting for you," stated the lanky boy as he closed the door deadlocking it in place.

Following the hallway, the hairs on Keebo's neck came to attention as the arcane forces flowed throughout the entire building. With Fleur in tow, he entered the office where they encountered others who had answered the Darkserpent's call.

"Ahh, Master Keebo, I see you have arrived and you have brought the Lady Tallbreeches. Good, good,'" stated Thucious as he sat calmly at his desk across from Edwyn who seemed to be slightly nervous.

"Yes sir, we are here. But I tried to talk her out of coming." stated Keebo as he was shot an annoyed look from the small rogue.

"I understand your fear young one, but fate requests that she accompany us this eve," stated the silver haired elf as he placed a hand on the young apothecary's shoulder. "And now I believe introductions are in order."

The master courier introduced them one by one. First he pointed to a dingy hide cladded Gnome by the name of Prints, who sat petting his oversized gray tabby. His skill at tracking would be useful in the tunnels. Next would be Jes the energetic Gnome apprentice of the Darkserpent himself. And finally Felixacis, the Darkserpent's adopted son, who was carefully arranging items on the desk.

Before we go, explained Thucious, we will need to be appropriately armed, for our adversary is not a mere rodent to be dealt with. Laid upon the desk were daggers and short swords made from the finest silver. Felixacis carefully began to pass them out according to each particular skill set each member possessed. And then Thucious took the young apothecary aside and handed him something else. Something special. It was a small ring, ornately carved, a small creature with wings and a tail made from silver and onyx.

"What's this for Thucious?"

"I created this for you, and have held it for what would seem this very moment, my boy," stated Thucious as he placed it in his small hand. "Although your wings have proved to be an invaluable tool, they may hinder you where we are going." "So I have crafted this ring's properties after my own. All you will need to do is place it upon your hand and rotate it slightly left."

The Hauflin didn't fully understand, but upon receiving the tiny onyx ring, a tingle shot down his spine, causing him to tremble slightly. The ring's enchantment was powerful. When the shiver passed, he slowly placed it upon his finger and rotated it slowly to the left. The ring's image slowly began to change, but that wasn't all. Keebo felt different, and the more the image changed the more different he felt. As he concentrated on the ring's image, its wings and tail slowly melted away leaving only the small body of a humanoid, a Hauflin. But the Imp also felt different, he felt a little off balance. Reaching behind him, he could no longer see his own wings or tail. They were gone. And looking around, his eyes met those of Fleur, who stood staring and jaw dropped.

The young apothecary turned to the Darkserpent with a hint of fear in his eyes.

"What's happening to me?" he asked the old silver haired elf as he tried to find his wings.

"Don't worry my lad." he said with a smile. "Just a little enchantment to make the tunnels more accommodating."

Keebo trusted the master courier, but they were still a part of him and he missed them. He also seemed a little off balance without their added weight.

Listening to their conversation, Fleur spoke up as to what she surmised would be the biggest problem.

"Master Darkserpent, sir. What about you two?" she asked while pointing to him and

Felixacis. "How are you going to make your way down into the tunnels, your Biggs?"

With a smile upon his lips, Thucious looked over to his son. With a nod, Felixacis started to shrink, his body changing into a leather clad, violet haired Gnome sporting an ornate rapier which was embraced by the ever smiling Jes. Next Thucious, rotated his own ring, allowing him to change his likeness into that of his Hauflin persona. Fleur and Keebo stared in amazement. Although they lived in a world of magic, it still wasn't that common to see people change their shape.

The group left the courier shop and headed toward the Whalebone entrance to the Burrows. Prints led the way, with his tabby, Pounce by his side. The group was passed by numerous rats that seemed to be flowing from all points in the city into the Burrows, as if an unseen piper called to them. Prints had to keep Pounce in check numerous times, as his companion eyed the numerous delicious four legged morsels. Following the Whalebone and the river of rats, the group carefully made their way down to the tunnels below. Exiting onto Boater's Way, they weaved their way, down into the deeper levels of the Burrows. The influx of vermin had caused the small folk of the Burrows to hole up in their homes, as the onslaught continued. The eclipse was growing closer and the rats were growing more erratic. Prints led them to the entrance that the deep Gnome had told them about. Taking only a moment for Thucious to cast his protective enchantments upon the group, they began their descent into the catacombs of spiraling tunnels.

The tunnels were dark, and as the party carefully made their way through them, Pounce stopped suddenly. The tabby stared cautiously as the tunnel forked ahead. Then the tabby let out a hiss, as a dire rat launched itself from the darkness ahead. A tangle of fur and claw filled the passageway as the two animals battled for supremacy. Prints yelled at his companion as he notched his crossbow. Drawing his aim upon the disfigured vermin, he once again whistled for Pounce to get clear of the shot. But the shot came too late, the dire rat's teeth tore deep into the tabby's neck, nicking the artery. Pounce pawed the dirt floor of the tunnel, eyes searching for his master. The tracker watched as the rat sank his teeth once again in his friend's lifeless body.

"Pounce" cried Prints as he dropped his crossbow and pulled out his handaxe. Overcome by rage he swung his axe, burying it deeply within the skull of the rat. Again and again he retrieved his axe, and repeatedly buried deep within the vermin until Felixacis stepped forward to control the hunter. Prints, fell to his knees as he rubbed the side of his departed friend, which had been with him since she was a kitten. Gaining his resolve, Prints once again took the lead as they made their way deeper into the tunnels.

Traveling with no further incidents, the group found their way to the newly excavated sub-basement. The pungent smell of incense and vermin now filled the tunnel, causing them to become slightly nauseated as the smoke created a cloud filling the top of the tunnel. Low murmuring could be heard as they neared the entrance. Felixacis carefully took the lead and maneuvered himself near the entrance. Waving the others forward, they carefully made their way towards the murmuring.

The basement had been filled with the squeaks of rats of all sizes and shapes, in the center the Worldwalker chanted over the weakened body of a seamstress that had been shackled to the dais in front of the rat shaped altar. The vermin seem to bob their heads to the rhythm held by the tainted slaves.

Moving into position, Fleur finally caught a glimpse of the altar and the female offering. "Mother" she loudly gasped, drawing the attention of the two largest rats in the chamber.

"Get them! I must finish the incantation!"

ordered Gillian as he drew his magical symbols in the air.

With a nod, the two largest rats started to transform, no longer four legged creatures. Now two wererats stood staring at the entrance of the basement. Pulling their rusty daggers from sheaths which had been strapped to their legs, they quickly headed toward the doorway. The two wererats, Tunks and Nip, had an unnatural thirst about them. Which they had planned to quench with the deaths of the intruders.

Prints and Felixacis met them at the entrance with their own blades bared. They had to make it through the entrance while trying to dodge the diseased ridden blades of the creatures. Prints' axe head buried deep into the shoulder of Nip, but the infected Gnome still advanced. The silver burned the creature, causing it to howl in pain, but still it trudged on until it could maneuver itself closer to the tracker. Behind the tracker, Jes curled her fingers into ancient arcane shapes, casting her enchantment. She yelled for Prints to move, hoping to clear up her shot. But that was the opportunity Nip needed. The slight distraction allowed the fiend to slide into the tracker's reach so he could bury his dagger to the hilt through Prints' ribs, wounding him. As the Gnome fell to the side, Nip looked at the red headed caster and smiled at her, licking his lips. But that too was all the time Jes needed. Finishing the last of the arcane symbols, her eyes glowed blue. From her outstretched hands, two arcane bolts shot from her finger tips, pummeling the wererat directly in the face, causing flesh and bone to shatter, leaving a smoldering hole in his skull.

This was the opening they needed. Thucious ordered Keebo and Fleur on into the basement determined to end whatever the Worldwalker had begun. Jes knelt trying to stop the river of blood flowing from the Gnome tracker as Felixacis answered the assault of Nip's partner Tunks, moving their battle farther into the tunnels. But as they passed into the basement, Gillian dropped to the stone floor with hands raised and yelled "Let it be done!"

The earth around the basement shuddered as a column of shadow and light broke through from the sky above. One could wonder as to what devastation was being done as the power pierced the streets above. And as the energy engulfed the altar and Sari, a wave of power emanated from the room, rippling in great waves, knocking all to their knees. They watched as Fleur's mother levitated from the dais screaming, her body retching and twisting as the power flowed through her, into her. The seamstress' limbs elongated in gross proportions, vaguely keeping the resemblance she once held. The essence of shadow seeping from her mouth and nostrils. Then the torches flickered out momentarily as an eerie wind blew through the tunnels out into the Burrows.

As the torches relit themselves, a being floated above the dais, shrouded in shadow stuff. Gillian found his legs, and knelt to the being with hands outstretched.

"Mistress, I humble myself before you," stated the Worldwalker. "Bless me, my goddess."

A voice echoed in the minds of all in the room. "I will my faithful servant in time, but first...." the voice grew silent, "but first we must deal with the unbelievers."

Gillian looked over his shoulder and stared at the Hauflins who delayed his reward. "You should not be here" he screamed. Turning around he raised the rod that was tied to his waist and unleashed a bolt of blue lighting toward them, but Thucious had finished his protective spell redirecting it to a mass of rats that had surrounded the altar paying homage.

Gillian growled as he again lifted his rod, only to see that the next bolt, too, was redirected towards another mass of vermin. The priest allowed the rod to once again rest at his belt. He had grown accustomed to allowing others to fight his battles, but he had fought his fair share of adversaries. Reaching beneath his cloak, he pulled two curved daggers free from their resting place and began to circle Thucious.

"You two take care of that creature," directed Thucious as he pointed to primeval god that hovered above the dais. "I will handle this rat." Then the Darkserpent pulled his own short sword and entered the fray.

Keebo and Fleur moved cautiously toward the creature that was enshrouded in the twisting shadows. Keebo's heart beat like the hooves of stampeding horses. He could feel the arcane energies webbing from his tiny heart through his veins. Keeping Fleur across from him, he had intended to flank the beast when suddenly he was attacked by tentacles of shadow. The shadows wrapped around him, throwing him to the ground. Again and again he was pummeled by the tentacles of shadow stuff. As he slashed at the unending darkness, he could hear Fleur pleading.

"Please let my mother go" stated Fleur who seemed to be frozen in place.

"My sweet daughter, why have you armed yourself against me?" the voice said as it reached into the rogue's mind. "Drop your arms, and stay with me. Don't you love your mother?"

"You're not my mother," stated Fleur as she

stood mesmerized as the elongated clawed hands beckoned to her. It wasn't her mother, was it, she thought. It couldn't be.

Keebo couldn't hear the entire conversation, but he knew in his heart that Fleur was being drawn deep into the clutches of the demon or whatever sort of being this was. Keebo watched as Fleur slowly gave way to the creature, slowly lowering her silvered daggers as she moved closer to it. A gleam of victory spread across the monster's face, as it reached its hands out to embrace her.

"No Fleur," yelled Keebo as he watched in horror as his love slowly moved within the writhing tentacles of shadow. The adrenaline had caused the arcane spider webs to spread over the entirety of his small body, which renewed his strength fighting the shadowy tentacles that held him at bay. Straining, he stretched his tiny fingers until he could reach the enchanted ring that denied him his true form. Rotating it to the right, the young apothecary quickly became the Imp, as the rings magic was no longer active. And as his wings burst forth from his back, he glanced to his love to see her now embraced by the creature most foul, but he also saw its true intentions. A spike made from shadows of the abyss now stood poised to strike down the young rogue, his love, from behind. With renewed vigor, the Imp forced the arcane energies that spider webbed his body to radiate out, weakening the shadows that bound him. And as he fought his way to his feet, he watched in terror as the barb speared his beloved in the back, piercing her leather armor and bursting forth from her chest. But it was not her screams that caught his attention then, but the screams of the beast. For when it pulled the spike out to render the rogue, Fleur had plummeted her own silver daggers into the gullet of the fiend. The creature screamed and clawed at the rogue, throwing her to the ground. Wrenching the daggers from its body caused holy fire to erupt from its wounds, consuming She Who Scurries. And as the holy fire spread through its veins, the room shook and was enveloped in the deafening screams of the outsider as she was sent back to the Abyss from which it came, leaving only the disfigured, charred remains of its host behind.

Gillian watched as his life's journey ended as abruptly as it had begun. He could hear the shouts of the other intruders coming down the tunnel, which he surmised that his two henchmen both failed as well. Turning, the Worldwalker nearly missed losing his own head as Thucious brought down his own short sword cutting deeply into his shoulder. Gillian had worked too hard to have his end met this way, and now surrounded, he would fight tooth and claw to survive, or have someone else fight for him. In a commanding voice, he called to his mindless ratlings, ordering them to attack the Darkserpent. From every corner of the room, they amassed upon the master courier, with nothing more than their fists to bludgeon him with. And while he was occupied, the priest began to transform into his rat form, and joined with the hundreds of others scurried from the basement in a wave of vermin heading towards the streets above. Boater's Way was engulfed by the tidal wave of rats that exited from the tunnels below. And Gillian was amongst them, the Worldwalker had survived too long to die in that filthy way, a hole in the ground. Following the forefront of the exodus, he stayed hidden within the multitudes as they burst forth from the Burrows and scattered throughout the city. Keeping his wits, Gillian knew he would not be able to hide within the city. He made his way to a galleon heading south; a Hauflin they would remember a rat, they wouldn't notice.

Fleur laid on the ground, her tiny chest heaving as each breath caused her pain. Keebo ran to her and held her tightly, his own hands trembling as he tried to staunch the bleeding.

"Please don't leave me, Fleur," he begged as held her tightly. "I need you."

Fleur just smiled at him as she looked into his

eyes. She could feel the pull, the tiniest tug as her time was ending. She felt lighter as every breath left her.

"It will be okay, my love. It is just my time," whispered the rogue as a small trickle of blood left her lips.

Keebo trembled as sorrow took hold, he began to be overcome as the feelings of loss overwhelmed him. Pulling her ever closer, he wrapped his wings around them both. His heartbeats became maddening as the glow from his tiny blue veins increased with each beat. The glow caused even the master courier to momentarily cover his eyes. And then, as if the light switch of the world had been turned off, the basement went dark.

"Indictus luminus" chanted Thucious, causing small orbs of light to illuminate the chamber. On the stone floor, now sat the rogue, holding the shallow breathing apothecary.

CHAPTER THIRTEEN

Keebo looked around the room once more. He would miss the Green Forest, but he knew he could always come back. It would always be home. It had been a month since his journey into the tunnels, the battle with the Worldwalker and whatever he had brought forth. He didn't remember much, but Thucious had filled in most of the details at the end. The last thing Keebo had remembered was holding her in his arms. The shadow spike piercing her. He had been a sleep for nearly a ten day, after that night. The altar destroyed and sub-basement sealed by stone and spell, the only thing left was the entranced ratlings. And even they had started to change back to themselves after the full moon's cycle had been completed. Thucious was sure it had to do with the disappearance of the Worldwalker though. He had scryed for him but as for now, his location was unknown, but Thucious would know if he returned to his city.

Picking up his new backpack, he slowly placed it over one shoulder then the other. It was odd to wear a normal sized backpack he thought as he rotated the silver and onyx ring on his tiny finger to the left. Thucious of course thought it might come in handy if the young apothecary kept it as well as the silver edged short sword. Stating sometimes the best protections we have are the secrets we keep. Fleur had thought so too.

"Keebs are you ready," came a voice from downstairs.

"On my way, love," Keebo stated as he took one more glance about the room and shut the door. Walking down the hall, he scratched the long haired calico tabby behind the ears as it kept trying to push against him. "Take care of the place, Patches, until I return." Taking a deep breath the young apothecary turned and looked down the stairs.

Edwyn and Fleur stood waiting at the bottom; Edwyn trying to convince her to pack more food, and Fleur shaking her head as she rested her hands on her hips. Smiling, Keebo descended the stairs, looking at them both.

"I will miss you little brother," stated Edwyn as he knelt down and hugged the Hauflin tightly.

"I will miss you too Edwyn. I'll be back, I promise." said Keebo as he watched a small tear form in the corner of his brother's eye. Edwyn smiled and retrieved a small burlap bound bundle from the table which he handed to his younger brother.

"What is it" asked the young apothecary as he slowly unwrapped the bundle.

Inside, tied neatly shut was a tome, with the symbol of the Green Forest carved into its leather bound cover. Keebo looked at his brother as a small smile crossed his lips.

"I thought you might need some help from time to time, little brother," stated Edwyn.

"You always take care of me," said Keebo, as he showed Fleur.

"And I always will," said Edwyn.

Edwyn walked the two Hauflins to the back door where Rosie and Bells sat chastising each other. Four riding dogs were harnessed and loaded with all they might need on their journey. Tucking the tome into the saddle bag of his riding dog, Keebo and his friends mounted up.

"Where to" asked Bells as he tried to keep his balance in the saddle.

"Where ever the road leads" answered Fleur as she smiled at Keebo.

"Where ever the road leads" stated the Imp.

– THE END –

22463255R00134

Made in the USA
Lexington, KY
22 December 2018